D0965949

Obsidian

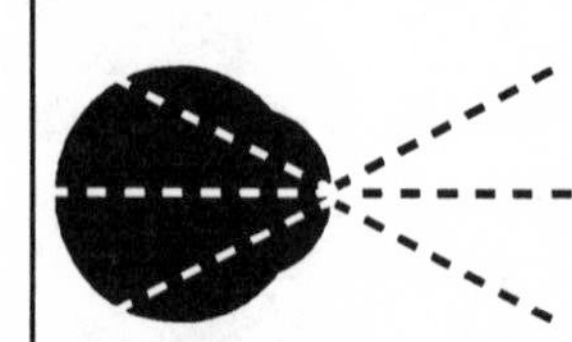

This Large Print Book carries the Seal of Approval of N.A.V.H.

Obsidian

Teagan Oliver

THORNDIKE PRESS
A part of Gale, Cengage Learning

Detroit • New York • San Francisco • New Haven, Conn • Waterville, Maine • London

This novel is a work of fiction. Names, characters, places, and incidents are either the product of the author's imagination, or, if real, used fictitiously.

Thorndike Press® Large Print Clean Reads.
The text of this Large Print edition is unabridged.
Other aspects of the book may vary from the original edition.
Set in 16 pt. Plantin.
Printed on permanent paper.

LIBRARY OF CONGRESS CATALOGING-IN-PUBLICATION DATA

Oliver, Teagan.
Obsidian / by Teagan Oliver.
p. cm. — (Thorndike Press large print clean reads.)
ISBN-13: 978-1-4104-0887-7 (alk. paper)
ISBN-10: 1-4104-0887-6 (alk. paper)
1. Coastal surveillance — Fiction. 2. Smuggling — Fiction. 3. Maine — Fiction. 4. Large type books. I. Title.
PS3615.L588O37 2008
813'.6 — dc22 2008027543

Published in 2008 by arrangement with Tekno Books.

Printed in the United States of America
1 2 3 4 5 6 7 12 11 10 09 08

For my Dad, for being my
very first hero.

ACKNOWLEDGMENTS

Writing is a mostly solitary profession, but becoming published is something that cannot be done alone. Thank you to all those who answered my endless questions along the way and my friends who offered creative suggestions for plotting all along this strange trip.

I would be remiss if I didn't acknowledge my children who love me whether I succeed or fail, and my husband who never hesitates to tell people that his wife writes romance.

My deepest thanks go to Julie Hyzy and John Helfers for believing in *Obsidian* enough to take the project on, and, also, I owe a great debt of gratitude and love to my Maine RWA family for their support, combined knowledge, and belief in me. Thank you all.

Prologue

Maybe it was the gentle rise of the wind lifting the hairs at the back of his neck and sending the chimes on his porch to swaying melodiously. Perhaps it was the absence of all other sounds except the buzzing in his ears that sent his senses into overtime. Whatever it was, something made him turn to look back.

Jamie watched as David throttled up the engine of his new twenty-six-foot Grady-White Offshore Pro and pulled away from the dock. Sunlight glistened off the hull of the boat, sending slivers of cascading light rippling into the water around it. The boat was a beauty and he was envious.

They'd spent the afternoon fishing off Minet Island with nothing but the traveling sun to remind them of the time. They hadn't caught much, but it didn't matter. It was a perfect day anyway.

Their good-natured rivalry knew little

bounds in their long-time friendship. Whether it was cars, boats, or women, David always prided himself on bettering him at everything. Today, he had succeeded.

Still, something wasn't right. David had been aloof and cocky, more so than usual and Jamie had attributed it to the feeling one-upmanship David was flying on.

Jamie set the tackle box at his feet and balanced the pole against his shoulder. The sky was turning orange with the last dying light and he waved as David's boat moved out and away from shore. It was his imagination working overtime. He'd been working too many long hours and seeing suspicion in everything. A hazard of a job he knew all too well.

Red sky at night, sailors' delight . . .

He turned back, reaching for his tackle box and the gentle buzzing in his ears increased to a blare of warning. The engine of David's boat began to throttle up as he got a few hundred feet out into the harbor.

Something was wrong. The scene played out in slow motion before him. His muscles tightened, his stomach clenched. Jamie reached out his hand to signal David, but it was too late.

A blinding flash fired before him, shaking everything with a resounding boom as the boat lifted from the water, exploding wildly — fire ripping from the deck. A cloud of black filled the sky as a rush of power flooded over him, throwing him to the ground. A shower of fractured fiberglass rained down upon him, fragments and hot ash searing his skin.

Pain and darkness washed over Jamie, swirling around him like an endless pool until he could do nothing but mutter a silent prayer and give in and sink away.

Chapter One

The Beachside Bar was not on the beach. It wasn't even close to a beach. Nor was it in any way the cultural experience the exotic name implied. It was a local hovel on a narrow back street in Key West, whose only claim to a beachside atmosphere was the fake fishing nets hanging from the ceilings and the seafood they served on chipped plates before unwary customers.

Jamie Rivard knew the place well.

He set his sunglasses up on his forehead, letting his eyes adjust to the darkness before sliding up to the bamboo bar. Nothing had changed since he had been here last. The same worn carpeting, the same faded beer signs hanging on the walls.

He motioned to the bartender for a beer and pulled a few dollars out of his wallet, dropping them onto the bar as the man slid the drink toward him. He eyed the other inhabitants in the mirror behind the bar.

A lone couple sat in the corner with eyes only for each other as their hands moved toward each other across the top of the table. Her honey blond hair and well-tanned complexion was something familiar, and yet, he couldn't quite put a name to the face. The man was heavy set, a bruiser of a guy with arms like tree trunks and an indistinguishable tattoo.

Jamie chose the table at the opposite corner, placing his back to the wall. Why in hell had McAlvey chosen this dump to meet? He could think of countless other places better suited to a discreet conversation. Other places with adequate lighting and passable food.

He sighed. His nerves were raw and on edge. But on the outside he remained calm. He checked his watch. McAlvey was late.

On the jukebox, an Eagles song ended and another, slower one started. The soulful lyrics were an aphrodisiac to the couple in the corner. They rose from their seats and started winding their way through the empty tables. The blonde draped herself against the hulk of a guy, tucking an arm around his waist.

"Jamie?" When he heard the husky pouting voice, vague memories filtered back to him of a long weekend spent drowning himself in tequila and mourning the loss of his best friend.

"Hello, Janna. How are you?"

She smiled a wicked, sweet smile that didn't go unnoticed by her male companion. He tucked the blonde closer.

"I'm just fine, honey. But, you are definitely looking much better than the last time I saw you."

"Yes, well being sober'll do that to you."

Beside her, her male counterpart puffed his chest at the familiarity.

"It's nice seeing you again." Jamie took a sip of his beer, hoping she would get the message and move on. "Take care, have a good evening." He tipped his beer in salute as the over-pecked male escorted her out.

Now, it was just he and the bartender, and still no McAlvey. From the back room the sound of a pool break clattered through the open doorway. Monday evening happy hour was not a high time for the Beachside.

The door swung open and a man walked in. He was wearing a flashy Hawaiian style shirt and a pair of white cutoff shorts with worn deck shoes. His short blond hair showed gray at the edges. He raised his sunglasses. There were lines of age surrounding his piercing blue eyes. He was well tanned, in his late fifties, and he looked like any other guy on the Keys, another Jimmy-Buffett-Wannabe. The only thing separating this man from a tourist was the large signet ring with a crest on his left hand. A casual bystander would never believe this man was a CO in the United States Coast Guard.

And McAlvey just happened to be *his* CO.

Jamie rose from his seat as much as from instilled formality than anything else. McAlvey didn't offer greetings. He nodded his confirmation of Jamie's presence and ordered his own beer.

"We aren't on ceremony here, Rivard." McAlvey pulled out the chair opposite him and motioned for Jamie to sit. They weren't at the base and the last thing either wanted was to call undue attention to themselves.

"I was expecting you a half hour ago." Jamie leaned back in his chair and appraised his CO. In the three years he'd been under his command they had never been much for making small talk.

"I was unavoidably detained." The bartender put the beer in front of McAlvey and he took a pull from it.

"Things happen." But things like this rarely happened to him. Jamie took another swig of beer and leaned back in his chair, bringing the front legs up off the floor.

"The scars are healing. How about the

leg?" McAlvey wasn't here for small talk and Jamie knew it. But he would play along and see what it was he wanted. He could be patient when needed. At least for a while.

"The leg is good. The scars, I'll have to live with."

They were charting some sort of uneasy territory here, setting rules for engagement for a battle Jamie had no clue about.

"You need a haircut," McAlvey said.

"I'll get one before I come back." Jamie took another sip of his beer to calm his nerves. It was warm. "For now, I don't need one."

McAlvey fidgeted with the bottle between his fingers. Moisture dripped down the side of the bottle and left rings on the plastic tablecloth. "You look better than the last time I saw you."

Jamie snorted. "The last time you saw me I was stinking drunk." Just another reminder of the blur after David's death. He cringed as he thought of how he'd acted. Despite what he let others think of him, it wasn't in his nature to act out. Hell, it wasn't in his nature to chase away things with alcohol, but for a while it had helped. Some.

"I should have had you detained. You had no place being on the base inebriated."

"Is that why you asked me here to meet

you? To discuss my past behavior?" The legs of his chair hit the floor with a thud. They both knew that wasn't the reason, but they had been dancing around the subject like a ghost that refused to go away.

McAlvey shook his head. "You're a loose cannon, Rivard. You've just been lucky and gotten away with it up until to now. I could have had you detained for your behavior."

"But you didn't." Instead, he'd sent him home with an escort and warned him not to set foot on the base until he was sober again.

"No, I didn't. But the only reason I didn't was because you were hurting." McAlvey eyes narrowed as he scrutinized him across the table.

"Yes, well I guess being put on enforced leave will at least make a person more rested." He may have been drunk, but he'd had a good reason. And the reason hadn't changed during the time he'd been away.

"It was either enforced medical leave, or find some other way of making you deal with David's death. Besides, you needed time to heal your leg and you were due some personal time. You haven't had any down time for two years."

"I've been busy." He couldn't help but let the sarcasm he was feeling come out in voice. He had been too busy to take leave because of his work. He'd spent the last two years chasing drug runners and smugglers. His last smuggling case had lasted six months and had netted a ton of cocaine and three major players. It had also been the last case he had worked on with David.

It was David who had pushed him into the Special Investigating unit. It was David that had loved the excitement and the adrenaline. They had been like brothers. Rivaling brothers, but brothers all the same.

"I want to know what happened to David. I want the truth."

McAlvey looked over the top of his beer at him. "You know those records are classified."

"And I've got the clearance. You can open them up for me."

"I can. But I won't." There was a tight edge to McAlvey's voice and Jamie had known McAlvey long enough to know that when pushed, his CO would push back. "I was hoping your time off would have calmed you down some."

"Hell, are you saying that the unexplained death of a friend wouldn't make anyone edgy?"

McAlvey shook his head. "I'm still your CO, Rivard. You would do well to remember that." But they weren't on the base and there was no place for decorum in this dingy little bar.

"I'm not giving up. I will find out what happened. Boats don't just explode without good reason." Jamie set the bottle on the table a little too hard, rocking the table with the force. He knew damned well there was more to David's death than what McAlvey was telling him.

"Even if you could see the report, it isn't going to tell you anything more than what I've already told you." He shrugged. "You should be thankful you weren't on board when it happened."

"I guess it's something David can't be thankful for."

McAlvey raised an eyebrow at him. "I didn't come here to debate."

Jamie doubted that very much. "You said in your message that you have information on David?"

"Of course, I can't tell you anything officially." McAlvey's eyes narrowed as he looked for some sort of a reaction from Jamie. Jamie didn't give any signals.

"Of course," he felt his nerves crank up a notch. "But off the record . . . ?"

"But off the record, we know that when David died he was close to making a break in the trafficking case he was working on."

"But something went wrong," Jamie said.

McAlvey nodded. "He was working on a lead, something about some activity by a Maine lobsterman named Case. David suspected that Case is the connection between the supplier and shipper, working as a go-between."

"So, if David had something, how is it you're backing off the investigation?" Jamie leaned forward, bracing the beer bottle between his fingers as he tried to assimilate the information.

"Because we've been ordered to refocus all of our manpower on Homeland Security. We've had reports of a credible threat. Everything else is to be put on the back burner."

"And you're telling me this why?"

McAlvey shrugged. His beer was empty. "Because I know that while officially this investigation is over, you would want to know why we aren't going forward with it."

There was more to it. McAlvey was giving him the information for a reason.

"Where was the tip from?"

"Chandler, Maine. I believe you know the area?" McAlvey leaned back, shrugging and settling his shoulders against the back of the chair.

Jamie did. "I am familiar with the area. My family has a summer cottage near there." He hadn't been back in fifteen years.

"Then, you know the area is ripe for activity. There are any number of places they can hide."

"And you think David was killed because he found out about this Case person?" Jamie twisted the bottle between his fingers, peeling the label off the bottle.

McAlvey's shoulders straightened as he leaned forward, pushing his weight against the edge of the table and motioning Jamie closer.

"I don't need to tell you that this is a delicate matter and I'm taking a risk telling you anything."

"But you're going to tell me anyway."

McAlvey leaned back in his chair again, assessing him. "I came here today to help you."

"And I appreciate your effort, but somehow I get the feeling there's more to this than what you're telling me."

McAlvey was silent for a moment. "I could be court-martialed for this."

They were going round and round. McAlvey wouldn't be here if there were a chance this would affect his career. Which only left him wondering what McAlvey was really after.

"How close was David to making a bust?" Jamie let the question slide between them.

"David intercepted a small time hustler making a gun exchange out of a pawn shop here in town. The guns were military issue, the same as were lifted from the base two months ago."

"So why not shut down the pawn shop and follow the leads from there?"

"We tried, but before we could get there the pawn shop was cleared out and there was no trace of them. This is not a small operation. All information indicates they are shipping the guns to a paramilitary faction in Northern Ireland."

"And this guy in Maine? How does he figure into it?"

"Suspicious activity was reported in Casco Bay. When the Portland base investigated they found a washed-up box containing guns. The same guns lifted from our base."

"So why didn't they investigate it instead of having it fall to the Special Investigative Unit?"

"Because of the nature of the case. This would look particularly bad if it were to get out that these were the Coast Guard's own guns."

"And we're being given a chance to redeem ourselves." By catching those responsible and keeping all traces of it from the press.

"Exactly. But there is one other thing. The woman who runs the local wharf is the sister of the same man in the information David intercepted. From what we can tell she has the only major access to and from the traffic going in and out of the harbor."

"Quite a coincidence." Jamie stared at McAlvey across the table. That niggling feeling he always got at the back of his neck whenever McAlvey was around was sending out shock waves the size of an earthquake. Either McAlvey was giving him his chance or there was more to the story than he was letting on.

"So, what is it that you're not telling me?"

McAlvey's eyes narrowed, glaring at him over the table. "Only that each time they received a report and tried to investigate, the activity stopped before they got there. It wasn't as if they knew they were coming and bailed. They were gone, all traces erased."

"Someone on the inside is leaking information." Jamie shook his head.

McAlvey nodded. "That would be the rational line of thought."

Jamie sat back in his chair for a moment.

He couldn't believe he was actually considering it. Was he really thinking about going back there after all these years?

"I want to take some of my vacation time," Jamie said.

"Well, I can't stop you. But if you should decide to take a trip to Maine keep something in mind, Rivard. If there is trouble on your so-called vacation, there won't be any immediate help available. You'll be on your own. But then, you always did work well on a solo basis."

"Sometimes, it is preferable."

Being a Special Investigating Officer didn't fit the confines of the rest of the Coast Guard. They were the few who were sent in when no one else could handle it. And they were the best at what they did. And David had been the best of them all.

"The specifics?"

McAlvey pulled a white, letter-size envelope from under his shirt and slid it across the table to Jamie. "You'll find all you need in here."

Jamie stuffed the envelope into the back pocket of his shorts.

"There is one more thing I should tell you." McAlvey looked down at the empty bottle in his hand. The hair on the back of Jamie's neck rose in anticipation of what he knew was coming next.

"There is reason to believe that David may have been involved with the disappearance of the guns. He had the opportunity with his special access and over the last few months, he was flashing around a pretty big amount of money. Money that couldn't be traced."

Jamie's stomach dropped to his knees. "Why didn't I hear about this?"

McAlvey shrugged. "It's only recently come to light. The investigation is just now getting under way."

"You swore to me that David wasn't working on anything when he was killed. I asked you and you denied it."

McAlvey shook his head. A worried expression creased his brow and his lips were tight and thin, and glued to his teeth. He looked around for anyone within earshot and then leaned toward Jamie across the table. "It was classified. The files were sealed."

And he had been lied to. There was more to this than what was on the surface. "You and I both know David wouldn't be involved with something like this. He wouldn't have done it and I'm going to prove it if it's the last thing I do."

"I would expect nothing less." McAlvey

stood up, tugging at the edge of his shirt and settling his sunglasses back into place. "Look Rivard, I know David's death has made it tough for you. But when this is all over I hope you can find some peace."

Jamie eyed the hand extended over the table to him. Something about it made his hackles rise. He ignored McAlvey's hand and after a minute the older man pulled it back, having the good graces to be somewhat embarrassed.

"You'll see me again when I'm through with this. Then, we'll deal with the rest of our unfinished business." He grabbed his beer, draining the contents into his mouth. He fought the bitter edge of lemon left at the bottom of the bottle. Kind of like the bitter edge of his life lately.

Solitude closed in on Shelby like an enveloping mist. The wind picked up, carrying across the tops of the trees, and the crack of the waves hitting the shore did little to soothe the ache filling her heart tonight.

It was an unusual habit she had, walking the shore at night; an especially strange habit for someone terrified of the ocean.

It was an unreasonable fear. Her conscious mind could clearly see she had nothing to be afraid of, but it was the dreams at night that filled her subconscious, keeping her from restful sleep, and chasing her — driving her to walk the beach like some haunted image in search of peace.

Shelby Teague shivered, pulling her thin coat closer around her. The warmth of the daylight had given way to the still cooler autumn nights. Maine in September was unpredictable at best. It could snow, or rain, or just about any other kind of condition in between.

She picked her way out to her own private spot high up on the cliffs. The jagged rocks stretched downward, slashing into the ocean and cutting into the darkened waves. She stayed back a safe distance, settling herself back against the rocks and pulling her feet up under her for additional warmth. She sat in silence for a long time as the wind buffeted her. She wouldn't find any peace here tonight.

It had been a whole year since Tommy's death. A year of change, a year of loss, a year of moving on alone.

She shivered as the cold seeped beneath the folds of her jacket. She should head home. It was getting late, too late to walk the beach alone. Besides, if she didn't return soon her uncle would get worried about her.

At first, the gentle buzzing she heard

above the wind was no more than a minor distraction, but as it increased, growing louder by the second, the noise filtered through her consciousness until she couldn't ignore it.

She put her hand to her ears, cupping them against the wind as she strained to determine the direction of the sound. Through the darkness the lights of a small plane emerged, dipping in toward the cove and skimming over the water like a large bird.

Stupid fool. This was not a night for anyone to be out flying. The plane circled the point, making a wide arc until it came around to the point once again. A large black form dropped from underneath, the image blurring in the night. Shelby held her breath as a splash sounded above the tremor of noise.

The whir of the engines increased as it turned, not going over the land, but heading out again low toward open water.

Shelby scrunched her eyes, scanning the waves for any sign of a package floating among the waves. Perhaps, it was her mind playing tricks on her. The darkness and the wind conspiring to make her think she had seen something. But what had she seen?

She pulled her coat back around her again

and began edging her way along the rocks, picking her way toward the water's edge. The rocks were slippery with seaweed and the jagged edges bit at her hands. Fear trampled through her mind, impeding her investigating. The sound of waves crashing filled her ears as she got as close as she dared and tried to look out over the surface of the water again. But all she could see were the sharp outlines of lobster buoys dancing in the waves. There was nothing there. No floating boxes. No bodies thrown in the ocean. Nothing.

It was her mind. It had to be.

She scrambled back to safety. She should go home. She had the distinct feeling that whatever she had seen tonight was not meant for her. The best thing to do would be to report it and let someone else investigate it in the daylight. But then, who would believe her?

Picking her way back across the rocks, Shelby took the wooded inland route toward home and civilization, deciding to come back in the morning. In the light, she would either find the evidence she was looking for, or realize this had all been a dream.

The last late summer twilight was going down over the Atlantic as Jamie eyed the envelope in his hands. The gritty sand dug between his toes and he wiggled them, liking the feeling against his bare skin.

It had been years since he had been to Maine. A lifetime.

Going back meant more than finding the answers behind David's death. It meant facing the demons he had been running from for years.

His cell phone rang and he scooped it up from the blanket beside him. The number was familiar. He punched the button.

"Hello Mother," he said, forcing a pleasant tone.

"Jamie Paul, it is high time you answered your phone. You've been ignoring my calls for weeks." Using his full given name meant she was pulling out the big guns.

"I'm sorry. I've been busy." A simple lie, but one meant to soothe her. He had no delusions that his mother would believe him. She knew all too well that the reason he didn't call had nothing to do with being busy.

"Are you healing? Are you eating okay? You could come home so I can take care of you." That was the last thing he needed. His mother was a kind soul who never gave up on his wandering ways or trying to repair the heart of the family that was lost when

Sam died.

"Mom, thank you, but you know I can't." Too much had come between him and his father to repair now.

"He's worried about you," she said quietly. Jamie chose to ignore this.

"I'm healing well, Mom. So well, that I'm heading back out on assignment. You may not be able to get a hold of me for a while." The less she knew the better.

"Jamie you can't run forever. At some point you and your father need to settle this. You should call him." But ten years of silence from his father couldn't be undone with a simple phone call.

"We'll see." But they both knew it wouldn't happen. "I've got to go, Mom. I'll call you as soon as I can." He gave her his best, most cheerful tone. "I love you."

"I love you, too." The sadness in her voice lingered long after he had hung up. With his brother's death his family had disintegrated. Now, the best for everyone would be for him to stay away.

He needed to focus on the job ahead. Between his thumb and forefinger, he pinched the envelope McAlvey had given him. Inside were very few answers to his questions. He knew the basics, and evidently, it was all he needed to know.

He took a lighter out of his pocket and lit it; pushing the flame against the paper and watching it burst with heat. It crumbled into blackened ash much the way David's boat had erupted into flames.

And that was an ominous thought for a man who believed heavily in coincidences.

Chapter Two

Shelby set down the plastic crate she was struggling with and held up a hand to shield her eyes from the sun as she watched her brother's boat move out past the moorings, heading toward open water.

She stretched, putting her hands at the small of her back as she moved. Her muscles ached from the heavy hauling, but it was a good kind of ache that came with the satisfaction of hard work.

She looked up at her store, an oversized cottage against the ledges above the wharf. The old roof was in need of new shingles and the siding had worn to a faded gray. But the painting and shingling would have to wait. Soon enough she would be busy getting ready for the winter. Before long, the snow would come and then they would all be stuck inside for the endless months of cold.

She threw her heavy, rubber gloves into

one of the plastic bins and headed up the path. The store was her domain, a virtual family landmark in Chandler. For eighty years, her family had tended to the people of Chandler, and now it was up to her to keep it going.

The gravel crunched beneath her feet as she made the short climb up the hill. Most days, she left the wharf operations to her uncle. She had some help in the store a couple of days a week, enough to free her to do things around the house, or keep the books. Still, some days she would have liked nothing more than to curl up in a chair with a good book and dream the day away.

Her uncle met her in the doorway. John Case's usual gentle gaze was guarded as he stared past her at the departing boat.

"I saw Josh head out."

Shelby shook her head. "He's done hauling for the day and he's gone to try some urchin diving."

As always when diving was mentioned, she thought of Tommy. But even with her husband's death her brother had no such misgivings about diving.

"Your brother is a stubborn fool." The trailing wake of her brother's departing boat settled into gentle waves. "He'll be hard pressed to find what it is he's looking for out there." His lips thinned into a long grim line.

"What do you mean?" Sometimes, she sensed caution in her uncle. He had taken on the role of protector, watching over her and her brother since their father's death.

"Josh takes too many risks. I don't need to tell you that diving is dangerous, especially when there's as little experience as he's got." He shook his head once again. "And Josh hasn't got sense enough to stay out of trouble."

"Don't worry, he'll be okay." Shelby gave her uncle's hand a quick reassuring squeeze.

But he was right. Josh was risking his neck to make a fast dollar, and he was forgetting the most important thing, diving was dangerous when the skill wasn't there. Something Tommy had found out, and Shelby couldn't forget.

She placed a hand on her uncle's shoulder. He turned to look at her, forcing the frown from his face and replacing it with a smile.

"He'll be all right," she said. He had to be.

"I hope you're right."

He looked down at her, for the first time taking in the orange rubberized coveralls and cotton shirt. He raised an eyebrow at her as she stepped back from his scrutiny.

"I'm not dressing to impress. I'm dressing to work. I can't haul buckets and barrels in a dress." She gave him a sigh. "What?"

"Nothing." The quiet in his voice made his words honey smooth. "All I'm thinking is we might do a bit more business if you had a dress on inside of those coveralls instead of one of your husband's shirts. Who knows you might even get a date once in a while."

Shelby shook her head. "You know I'm not looking to date. And even if I were, it wouldn't be anyone in Chandler."

"That's good," her uncle chuckled. "Because with that outfit the only thing you're likely to attract is a bunch of seagulls."

Shelby propped the lid of the tank up over her arm while the latch dug into the soft spot between her shoulder blades. Inside the tank, her head was filled with the noise of the ailing pump as she struggled to keep the tubing in place. This was the second time in as many months she'd had to replace the pump on the holding tank. She should be a pro at it by now.

Her uncle's words about her clothes had struck a nerve in her. It had been a long time since she had paid any attention to her looks, never doing more than a quick glance in the mirror as she headed out the door. There was little use for fancy dresses in her line of work, but still his words irked her. So much, she had put away the coveralls for now. At least until she needed them again.

She looked down at the water below her in the tank. A lobster with its spiny antenna eyed her back, waving a banded claw in her direction.

"Watch it, or you'll be lunch." The lobster backed away as if he had sized up his opponent and found her lacking.

Her hand slipped off the black, rubber filter tubing. Shelby fumbled against the edge of the tank as she fought with the slippery hose.

The place was starting to fall apart around her. She did her best, but sometimes it was much more than she could handle on her own. Someday, it would be nice to have someone to share some of the duties around here with her. Her uncle did his best to help out where he could. But at times like this, it would have been nice to have someone to share the responsibilities.

She repositioned her feet in the gravel, trying to reach a little further into the tank. Her soft-soled boots slid against the rocks and she struck out to steady herself. Her hand came down hard in the tank, splashing water and sending up a soaking spray into her face. Water dripped off her bangs and into her eyes. Great, just what she needed.

"Can I help you with something?"

Her head hit the underside of the tank lid with a thump and she pulled back, letting the lid slam down behind her. She looked up, half expecting to see her uncle's stout form. Instead, she froze in mid-motion, her shirttail still gathered in her wet hands as water dripped down her cheek.

He was tall and long, lean and wiry, a good five or six inches taller than most of the men she knew. She dropped the edge of her shirt.

The stranger wore well-washed jeans, faded to a summer sky blue. His T-shirt was blinding white, in stark contrast to the mass of dark hair hanging in waves just above his collar. She would have remembered someone who looked like him.

"May I help you?" She tilted her head to the side and squinted against the glare of the afternoon sun.

A pair of sunglasses hid his eyes. The black metal frames outlined a burst of bright colors. She looked past him to the motorcycle he had parked next to her truck. A large canvas duffel bag was tied to the back of the bike and the flashy paint job was covered with a layer of road dust.

No, she definitely would have remembered someone like him.

"I believe I was offering to help you. You looked like you could use some."

Shelby smoothed her hands against her jeans self-consciously. The rough texture rubbed beneath her fingers and suddenly she was very aware of her less than feminine appearance.

"Thank you, but I'm fine." Her words sounded sharp even to her own ears. Maybe her uncle was right. Maybe she was becoming uncivilized.

He smiled. "I can see." He pulled a handkerchief from his back pocket and held it out to her. "Here, take this. I don't have a towel on me, but this should help."

Shelby took the scrap of blue fabric, wiping at the water on her hands and her face.

He waved her off as she reached out to hand it back. "Keep it. It looks as if you might need it again." She wasn't sure if she should be insulted by the stranger, or pleased at his politeness.

He raised his sunglasses, resting them against his hair. He had nice eyes, a smoky cross of gray and blue. But there was a weary edginess in his gaze that kept the smile on his lips from reflecting in his eyes.

A thin, white scar ran from the corner of his eye to disappear beyond his hairline. It did nothing to distract from the man's good looks. Instead, it intensified the air about him and added to his somewhat dangerous appeal. Shelby widened her stance, bracing herself against the sudden weakness in her legs.

He raised an eyebrow at her, giving her a one-sided charmer smile, a mere quip of the lip. But it was enough to step up her pulse a notch.

She really did need to get out more.

"I'm looking for a job and I was told I should try here." His voice was slow and languid, sending a fresh shudder up her spine. It held a slow caress of a southern twinge that slid down the length of her and settled at her toes. It was sultry, deep and not from Maine.

He moved closer, covering the distance between them in a few easy steps. His height blocked the sun from her face and allowed a rather up close and personal look at his features. He was handsome.

Still, he was a stranger and in a town the size of Chandler, there were few who welcomed outsiders, especially ones that looked too pretty to get themselves dirty doing hard work for a living.

"You'll be hard pressed to find work around here unless you know something about baiting traps, or hauling lines."

"And you don't think I'm suited for it?" He gave her a hard unnerving gaze that started at her feet and worked upward to settle upon her face. He smiled the same slow, one-sided grin he had offered before. "Yes, well, looks can be deceiving can't they? When I pulled up I thought you were a man." His words slid between them before he added, "But you are definitely *not* a man."

Sensibility said she should be outraged at his chauvinistic attitude. But she was finding it hard to muster up anything beyond the squeak that threatened to come out of her throat. After all, she was judging him on appearance. Fair was fair.

She reached behind her in the lobster tank for her forgotten pliers. Maybe if she dismissed him he would go away and leave her alone. But no such luck.

"Do you know where I might find the owner? I was hoping he might know where I could pick up a job on a boat."

Shelby slammed the lid down on the tank. Water splashed inside the tank, but she didn't care. It was a natural question and one she got often. So, why was it the same words from this stranger should get her ire up?

"Try again." She said through clenched teeth. Any trace of humor she may have had vanished. Strangers tended to think the fishing industry was a male-dominated occupation. They couldn't, or wouldn't, even begin to imagine anything different.

"Excuse me?"

Shelby turned to look out over the wharf and the green-gray water hitting against the docks. At that moment, she wanted to be anywhere but where she was.

"I own this place."

Instead of looking uncomfortable, he smiled. "That's great! So you can help me."

Shelby rolled her eyes. "Look, you don't know me and I don't know you. So, let's cut through all of this shall we? If you're looking for a job on one of the boats, then you should be talking to the boat owners."

"In other words, I offended you and you have no intention of helping me." He raised his chin a bit.

"Are you always this honest, Mr. . . . ?"

He smiled again. "It's Rivard, Jamie Rivard. And my intention was not to offend you, only to offer help."

"Well, Mr. Rivard, while I appreciate your

offer of help, I am not the person to help you. I would suggest that if you are truly interested in a job on one of the boats you should speak with the owner of the *Crosstide.* It's moored down off Pine Ledge Road."

He nodded at her. "My thanks to you for the help. It is much appreciated."

Shelby held up her hand. "I wouldn't thank me yet. You haven't gotten the job." Deciding that this was the best time to make her exit she turned and headed for the store.

"Are you always this prickly, or is it only with strangers?"

Shelby stopped, turning back to look at him.

"Mr. Rivard, I will give you fair warning. Strangers are not always accepted in Chandler. There are people that have lived here most of their lives and are still considered from away. So, if you are looking for some fun for a few months, you need to keep a few things in mind. For these people, this is their life. This is their income, and they take it very serious. They rarely trust anyone they haven't known since they were in diapers and if you cross them just once you're sunk. So, if you are still up to the job, then go. I have work to do."

Finished with her tirade, Shelby turned

and walked as steady as she could manage through the door to the store. Her knees and hands were shaking and her teeth hurt from clenching her jaw.

She had plenty of work to do and it didn't entail sitting around jabbering with some ego-inflated, tight-jeans-wearing tourist with an attitude.

The *Crosstide* was tied to the wharf when he pulled up. From the garbled directions he'd gotten from a neighbor down the road, this had to be it.

A thin wooden boathouse was settled against the ledges. The rough shingles and tin roof did nothing to hide the fact that a good, strong tide and some hurricane force winds could wash it out to sea.

Jamie pulled his motorcycle up outside the boathouse and cut the engine. He sat there for a moment letting the quietness sink into his body. He loved his motorcycle. It was fast and fun, but the sound of it could wake the dead. What he had thought would be a nice trip up the coast had constituted nothing more than a perpetual pounding headache and a sore leg. Still, it was nothing a good night's rest and some fresh salt air couldn't cure.

The gritty, whining crank of an engine trying to be started pulled him from his thoughts.

He had something to do and he'd better get it over. He knew from his own personal experience, the woman was right. People in these small Maine towns were not always open to newcomers. They tended to guard their privacy closely. And nothing could change the fact that he was an outsider.

Swinging his leg over the motorcycle, Jamie made his way down the narrow, pebbled path to the wharf, his feet sliding against the small pebbles.

The weathered planking of the dock was piled high with gear, leaving only a small pathway to pass through. As he approached the *Crosstide,* the sound of the engine grinding filled the air.

"Hello. Anyone here?" No one was on deck.

A muffled curse preceded him, as a man made his way out of the boat housing, wiping his greasy hands on a rag. Jamie figured him to be in his late fifties. He had broad shoulders and big hands and the roughened look of someone who made their living on the water.

"Can I help ya?"

Jamie straightened up, grabbing at the sunglasses he'd pushed to the top of his head. Fishermen are a complicated breed, independent to a fault and not afraid to judge a man. He was just hoping for some leniency. He reached out a hand in greeting and put on his most winning smile.

"The name is Jamie Rivard."

The man looked down at Jamie's hand and back up again as he continued to wipe his hands on the rag. Jamie dropped his hand, stuffing it into his pocket.

He felt like a school kid squirming in the chair in the principal's office.

"Are you the owner?" Jamie motioned toward the *Crosstide.*

The man shook his head. "One of 'em."

Having made it this far, he pushed on.

"I was told by the lady at the store that you might be able to tell me where I could get a job on a boat."

He stopped wiping his hands and looked at Jamie again, sizing him up.

"Shelby sent you?" He shook his head, dismissing him. "You don't look like you could do the job." It wasn't a question, more a statement of fact.

Jamie hadn't felt this uncomfortable since the nuns at St. Catherine's had hauled him before the Mother Superior for smoking in the bathroom. He cleared his throat and tried standing a little straighter. He had to convince him he was capable.

"I've got experience working on a boat."

"And what kind of experience would that be?" The older man grabbed at the large, blue bait barrel at his side and began half-rolling, half-dragging it to the back of the boat.

"I worked on a shrimp trawler off Louisiana."

"Louisiana, huh?"

Jamie nodded.

"Never been there. Besides — " He looked Jamie in the eye this time as he shook his head. "Not quite the same up here. You wouldn't like it much."

Their conversation, much as it was, had ended as soon as it had begun. The man grabbed a hose and started spraying down the deck. Jamie was in a spot. He needed this job if he were going to have a cover.

"You're looking for someone to help out, and I'm looking for a job. It seems like a good fit to me."

The fisherman just shrugged and looked over at Jamie again and then back at the job at hand. He couldn't help wondering what it took to impress a man like him.

"I've already got a teenager who goes out with me. But he's got himself a job in town at one of those fast food joints. I'm looking for someone to go out with me a few times a week. I fish a hundred traps or so, and I only go out about four days a week. I head out early mornings most of the time and I'm back in the afternoon. You'd have to be getting up pretty early to work with me."

He shrugged as though he was already counting Jamie out. "Besides, I imagine you're looking for full-time money so you won't be wanting this work." Finished with the deck, he wound the hose in a circle on the deck.

Jamie looked at the boat. Working a couple days a week would be just the right cover. He'd have some time to look around and get a feel for what was going on and have a legitimate reason for being here. But, if he were too anxious, he'd never give him the job.

"You having problems with the engine?"

"Do you know anything about motors?" He motioned in the direction of the engine compartment. "I can't get the blasted thing to turn over. She sparks, but won't catch."

Jamie launched himself over the side of the boat. If this were what it was going to take to get a job, he would do it. Besides, they had taught him a thing or two about marine engines at the Maritime Academy. So what, if he wasn't known for being mechanically inclined. How bad could it be?

He moved into the small engine compartment. The thick odor of gasoline hung in the air and he coughed as it filled his lungs. At least he'd managed to find the engine. That was good. Now, if he could bluff his way through, he might just be able to convince the guy to give him the job.

The obvious answer would be a flooded engine and it would take some work before the lines drained and the engine could be started. He looked around at the cramped quarters. It was clean and well tended. The man took pride in his equipment.

Jamie fiddled around for a few minutes checking out the wires and valves on the engine. It looked pretty close to the engine in his Thunderbird. He'd had a problem once with one of the lines. Maybe that was the case with this engine. He pulled off the air intake line and blew through tubing. No obstacles there.

He went on and checked the carburetor, but it appeared to be in order. So much for the obvious. He wasn't going to be able to dazzle the man with his mechanical abilities. He had none. He was already at the end of his limited knowledge and he still had no idea why it wouldn't start.

"Try and turn her over again." He called out. Maybe if he could just hear what the engine was doing, he might be able to guess what was wrong.

There was a click, click and then a low whining noise.

"That's more than I got before. At least there's some improvement."

Jamie began fiddling around and checking the points, but nothing looked out of place, except him.

"Did you say that her name is Shelby?" He looked up over the motor.

The other man eyed him for a moment before nodding his head. "Shelby Teague."

"She and her husband have a nice place there. It must keep them quite busy."

The other man shook his head. "Shelby runs the place all by herself and does a right good job of it. It hasn't been easy since her husband passed, but she does it anyway." There was appreciation in his voice. It was a high compliment and it was easy to see that his kind of appreciation wasn't easily won.

Jamie filed away the knowledge for later as he checked everything over once again. Running his fingers over the connecting wires, he checked the spark plugs and motioned for him to try the engine again.

This time there was more chugging and a few whining noises, but it still wouldn't catch.

On a hunch, Jamie pulled the gas line, draining the small amount of fluid into an old coffee can, and checked it for blockage. There was a small obstruction; a few particles of sand filtering out of the tube when he shook it, but not enough to kill the engine. It could, however, hamper the fuel intake.

Once he had cleared the tube, he bent it back into place and connected it. That was when he made another discovery. A small cut severed halfway through the line near the connectors. It was a clean cut, with no signs of wear.

If this had been different circumstance, he would have suspected foul play. But maybe he was just testing him. Or maybe he really didn't know about it and had just missed the cut line.

"There was some sand in the line, but my guess is it was this." He handed him the line and he took it, inspecting the cut.

He shook his head. "That's the last time I buy my gas and parts over at Guthrie's. Why that no good bait-for-brains. I should have known he would sell me a bad part. Cripes, he probably sold it to me on purpose."

Jamie stepped out of the engine housing and stood up, shaking off the crick in his back. His leg ached from being crouched in the small compartment, but he chose to ignore it. The last thing he needed was for his perspective employer to notice his injury. Any sign of perceived weakness could be a reason not to hire him.

Jamie edged his way to the side of the boat and levered himself up and over the side onto the dock. The other man followed, scratching his head in thought.

"I appreciate you finding it. I guess I missed it."

Jamie shook his head. "You would have gotten it sooner or later."

He held out his hand to him. "Name's John Case."

Jamie looked at John's hands. His long callused fingers were cracked and thick. One fingernail was almost gone.

Out of the few leads McAlvey had given him, John Case topped the list. And Case had dropped into his lap and he hadn't even known. Now, all he had to do was figure out what an Irishman with no past history to speak of was doing in Chandler, Maine, and acting as though he'd been here all of his life.

Jamie reached out for the offered hand.

"So, does this mean you're going to hire me?"

John looked out past the boat, toward the water, weighing his options, keeping his cards close to his chest. "You're hired. But I have one question."

"And that would be?" He was ready for anything. If he had to, he'd give a skill demonstration. Hell, he'd work a week for free if it meant he could get close to Case.

John nodded at Jamie's feet. "Are you gonna work in those fancy boots, or are you gonna get yourself some real ones like mine?"

Jamie looked down at his worn cowboy boots, with their smooth soles and raised heel. They were out of place with John's black rubber boots. "I guess I'll just be buying myself some of them fancy ones like yours."

John laughed, clamping a hand on Jamie's shoulder. "And I know just the place you can get some. We start on Monday, bright and early. Be here at five, or I leave without you."

Chapter Three

By the time Shelby had finished putting the kettle on the stove for her after-dinner tea, the afternoon light was turning to an evening dusk outside the kitchen window. Her uncle had gone down to the wharf to make sure everything was set for the night and she was left to bear the quietness of the vacant house. She hated it. It was much too quiet.

She had given in to the lingering Indian summer warmth and donned a pair of cutoff jeans with frayed edges and a sleeveless top, leaving her arms bare to feel the cooling breeze.

It had been quite a day.

All afternoon she'd been distracted by the image of Jamie Rivard. It sounded trite, like a reference to a country song, but she couldn't get his slow, easy smile out of her mind. Or the way he had been relaxed, even polite, as she had given him a dressing down.

Her cheeks flared with heat. She was rude to him, more than he deserved. But there was something about his attitude that made her uneasy.

She piled the dishes into the sink and started running the water into one side, adding the dish soap as her mind wandered.

Josh wasn't in yet, and it was getting late.

And because he was late, she couldn't help thinking about that night a year ago when she had waited for Tommy to come back. The hours had gotten later and later, with no sign or word of him, or his boat. And she had been left waiting and hoping for the best and somehow knowing the worst was yet to come.

At first, she hadn't worried too much. Tommy had been late before. He was a hard worker, always pushing himself to pull in one more string of traps. But that night she spent hours standing at the window looking out over the water, watching for him as all the other boats came in for the night. And then she had called the Coast Guard.

After hours of searching, they'd found his boat circling unmanned. Everything on the boat, all of the gear and the safety equipment, had been found intact, except for his diving gear, but no Tommy. Finally, after two days of searching, the search and rescue had turned into a recovery mission.

Eventually, they had just given up altogether. The official determination was recklessness on Tommy's part. They concluded that he had been diving alone and his inexperience had caused him to drown. It was all very cut and dried. All very polite. And, all very devastating.

But their logical answers had done nothing to ease her mind, or her grief. At twenty-six, her husband was gone and she was a widow. Three weeks later Tommy's body washed up on a nearby island and the Coast Guard's determination had been confirmed. Tommy's carelessness had taken him away from her.

Now, Josh had decided he could make money faster by diving and there wasn't a thing she could do to stop her headstrong little brother. She couldn't go on trying to protect him forever. At some point, she was going to have to let him make his own mistakes no matter what the consequences.

She looked out the window at the shoreline. From her window she had a good view of the whole harbor as the lights flickered on, one by one, in the windows of the houses along the shore.

Most of the boats were on their mooring

with only a few left tied to the dock, cleaning up and preparing for the next day. Still, there was no sign of her brother.

"Damn it, Josh. Why do you have to be so stupid? Why do you always have to take risks?" But the only answer was the shrill whistle of the teakettle sounding its readiness.

Jamie guided his bike back along the narrow road that ran along the shoreline.

Things settled early in Chandler. Only a few hardy souls were out walking, raising a hand in greeting to him as he roared past. But most just stopped and stared.

He followed the directions scrawled in coarse handwriting on the clip of paper in his hand. At the head of the cove he turned south, following along to where the road turned to well-traveled gravel.

He turned into the driveway in front of a rather unimposing two-and-a-half-story, shingled house. It wasn't any one particular style, more a jumble of the many additions and afterthoughts the house had been subjected to over the years. Rooftops stuck out at odd angles, a small dormer here, a shed roof there. The weathered shingles and painted trim were so typically New England in style.

He looked closer. The paint on the trim was raised and rippling and some of the shingles were cracked and warped. The house needed some work. It wasn't fancy by any stretch of the imagination, but with a little luck, it would be a place to rest his head while he was here.

He parked his bike under the shelter of a large oak tree, where a hedge of wild rose bushes ran a boundary line the length of the property.

Swinging off his bike, he grimaced as he put all of his weight on his leg. He muffled a curse as he put a hand on the bike to steady himself. Maybe he was pushing it to expect his leg to perform without a hitch after such a short time. The trip had taken its toll on him and now he was paying for it.

He turned to unstrap the cords holding his gear in place. It was a small pack, only the essentials. He didn't plan on staying long enough to need much, just long enough to wrap up the case.

Behind him a door creaked and slammed shut. Jamie straightened, turning away from the pack he was busy untying. But his fingers stilled on the binding cords.

Shelby Teague stood barefoot in the grass, watching him, and for the second time that day, Jamie found he was incapable of forming an intelligent greeting.

"What are you doing here, Mr. Rivard? Come to insult me some more?"

High green blades of grass covered her feet. Her hair hung down, curling softly against her shoulders. She took a few steps, stopping just a few feet in front of him.

Jamie held tight to his bag, not daring to move a muscle for fear he would say or do something that would scare her off and prove to her that he really was a complete idiot.

"John Case sent me, he told me you had a room for rent."

"And I'm supposed to rent to a total stranger?" She brushed at a wisp of hair that fell forward into her eyes.

"Look, I know we didn't hit it off well at our last meeting, but I would appreciate the chance to change your opinion of me."

She nodded. "Mr. Rivard, you have no idea what my opinion of you truly is. Granted, you were on the receiving end of my little tirade, but I can assure you that I rarely hold a grudge."

"Point taken, still, I would hate to anger the landlord." And run the risk of her asking him to leave.

"I wouldn't worry, Mr. Rivard. My uncle

wouldn't have told you to come here if he didn't think you were safe."

Fading sunlight cast a halo of light on her hair. Her face was free of make-up and her nose was sprinkled with a ring of freckles that laced her high cheekbones. Gone were the faded jeans and loose shirt that hid her body. Instead, she wore shorts that clung like second skin and showed off her long legs. Her oversized shirt had been replaced in favor of a blue tank top that left her shoulders bare and smooth. She had great shoulders.

Jamie stood motionless, his brain frozen, as he watched her close the few remaining steps between them. She reached for the bag, pulling it from his fingers, and clutching it in her own. She held it in front of her, the dark leather contrasting with her pale skin. She could have walked up and taken his gun from him and he wasn't sure if he would have been able to stop her.

She reached a hand out in greeting. "We haven't formally met. I'm Shelby Teague."

Jamie willed himself to raise his hand and place it in hers. Her touch was smooth and warm against his skin. "Please, call me Jamie."

She frowned. "Is that short for something?"

Jamie shook his head. "Only to my mother: she calls me Jamie Paul, but she usually reserves it for when I am in trouble. Most of my friends call me Rivard."

She laughed, "I think I'll stick to Jamie."

She looked down between them and his gaze followed hers. He had yet to release her hand. He dropped his grip, pulling it away with a quick motion. The imprint of her touch burned against his palm, making his fingers itch.

He was acting like some hormone-induced idiot without a brain to rely on and all of his training was flying out the window.

He was so used to knowing the right words to say to a woman. But then, Shelby Teague wasn't like any woman he had ever met before.

"You must have impressed my uncle." Her soft words and implied tone made him raise an eyebrow at her. A ghost of a smile traced her lips.

"Why would you say that?"

Her gaze traveled down from his boots to his jeans and on upward to his T-shirt. He was standing inspection here and the last thing he wanted to risk was having her think he wasn't a good bet.

"Because he's very protective of my brother and I. Did he give you the job?"

"I start Monday bright and early."

"You work very fast, Mr. Rivard."

"I've never been known for taking it slow." He flashed her a smile and motioned toward the house. "Shall we?"

She nodded. "I'll show you to your room. Room and board is eighty dollars a week with dinner included. You get the run of the kitchen. But you have to fix your own breakfast and lunch since I'm usually down at the store. I don't do the laundry for the boarders, but there is a washer and dryer in the basement if you want to do them yourself. I only ask that you keep quiet and if you want to have night visitors that you don't do it here."

"Night visitors?" He gave her his best innocent look.

Shelby's cheeks stained a pale rose pink as she raised her chin to look him in the eye. He had to give her credit. She had a lot of nerve.

"You know . . . company . . . at night?" She shifted in front of him and he stifled a grin. It was a rather old-fashioned rule, but then he wasn't here to have visitors, night, or otherwise.

"You mean female visitors? At night?"

He felt bad for making her uncomfortable, but there was something about her that made him want to tease her, if even just a little.

"Exactly. Now if you agree to the terms I'll show you around."

"Lead the way." He took his bag back from her. It was best he hold onto his own gear. He didn't want to risk making her suspicious when he hadn't even gotten through the door. But he couldn't risk it, if she were to see just what was in his pack.

"I could have carried that for you." Her smile disappeared.

"I'm sure you could, but my mother taught me that a lady should never be allowed to carry packages themselves. She'd have my hide if she thought I let you carry my things. Call it my southern hospitality training coming through."

She faltered for a moment, motioning at his bag. "Is that all you have?"

"I tend to travel on the light side. There isn't much you can pack on a motorcycle." He always traveled light. It made it easy when he needed to leave in a hurry. He had been in enough shaky situations to know you never carry something with you that you can't afford to leave behind.

"If you want, you can store your bike in the garage out back. It isn't much. My brother, Josh, keeps his tools and nets out there, but I don't think he'll mind if you store your bike there."

"I appreciate the offer. Thank you." He followed her toward the steps.

"It's no problem. When my brother gets in I'll have him get the key for you. He's should be in any time now." She glanced toward the shoreline. Even the harbor was quiet now. "Besides, when he sees that bike of yours, you won't be able to keep him away from it."

Jamie stored this away in his memory for later. It was perfect. When Josh did show up, he would be in a perfect position to observe him without bringing too much attention to himself.

And he would be waiting.

But there was a note of caution in her voice.

"Is something wrong?"

She let out a sigh, glancing at the shoreline once again. "No. It's just that my brother's been out diving this afternoon and I haven't been able to raise him on either the phone or the radio. I'll rest easier when he makes it back to shore and I know he's safe."

He watched her walk toward the house ahead of him, her hips swaying back and forth as she picked her way across the yard. He liked watching her. There was something oddly satisfying in the subtle sensuality of her movements, or the way she moved her head to the side when she spoke. Her movements were both unconscious and graceful.

He hoisted the narrow strap of his pack over his shoulder and followed her up the narrow wooden steps. The screen door screeched as it slammed behind them.

The small kitchen had a fifties look. Black and white tiles covered the floors, and the counters were an interesting shade of green Formica with a gray speckled tinge. Cookie-cutter trim edged the wooden cabinets and the wallpaper had a dancing teapot motif. It was outdated, small, but clean.

"Well, this is the kitchen." She pulled open the heavy refrigerator door. The light cast a pattern on the linoleum floor. "You can keep whatever you want on the bottom shelf, but I would suggest you mark it because my brother isn't too selective. He'll eat anything that gets in his way." She let the door swing shut and then turned back giving him a smile. He found himself smiling back.

"I suppose growing boys do have a way of eating a lot."

"Growing? My brother is twenty-five years old. I was hoping someday he would grow out of it. But now, I just hope he will find a wife who will feed him, so I won't have to anymore."

He laughed and she laughed with him and he found himself watching her face, watching to see her expressions. He liked the way she dipped her head down when she laughed and the way she raised an eyebrow at him when she was trying not to look at him.

She ushered him on, through the small dining room with a round oak table and several mismatched chairs scattered around it. Papers filled the top of the table.

"Sorry about the mess. I like to bring home the paperwork from the store and spread it out on the table to work on it." She gave a shrug as she moved on. "We eat in the kitchen now, so there isn't much need for the big table."

She led him through the dining room to the front of the house. The living room was furnished simply with a couple of overstuffed chairs, and a large brown couch that didn't go with anything else in the room.

"Come on, follow me and I'll show you the bathroom and your room."

She led him down a narrow hallway lined with doors, pointing out a small bathroom, decorated in pink and black tiles. A large, claw-foot tub filled one corner of the room and a shower stall occupied the other. The shower curtain was decorated with tropical fish floating on a blue tinted sea. It was very homey and very comfortable.

"You are welcome to use this bathroom, or the small one upstairs, but I think you'll find this one a little more private. The only other person you'll have to share it with is my uncle." She opened the door opposite the bathroom, facing the front of the house.

His room was the same as the rest of the house, small, comfortable and quiet. The single size wooden bed was covered with a soft, washed quilt of colorful patterns. The rug on the floor was a braided design of honeyed hues that matched the wide plank flooring.

"It isn't fancy, but it's a good room. I put you here on the first floor so you could have privacy. My uncle's room is just down the hall. So if you hear any creaking floorboards at night, it's probably him. He likes to take late night walks."

Jamie set his bag on the end of the bed and turned around in the small room. Over the bed was a large window overlooking the front lawn to where it sloped down toward the water. It was a million-dollar view.

"If you need anything, my room is at the head of the stairs and to the left. You can store your stuff in here for now." She motioned toward the upright dresser in the corner. "But if you need anything else, just let me know."

The dresser would be more than enough to suit his simple needs.

"Well, I'll leave you to your things. I'm sure you'll want to get yourself settled. There is some lemonade in the refrigerator if you get thirsty later."

Jamie shook his head. He needed to get his bearings and the sooner he did that the faster he could accomplish what he was sent to do.

"I think I'll just get some shut-eye for the night. It was a long ride here and I'm tired to the bone."

"Oh." Her mouth formed a small round circle and his gaze was drawn to her lips. They were sensual lips. They were lips that didn't need the aid of lipstick to look soft and sexy.

And she was looking back at him; her eyes mirroring the round shape of her lips, surprise dawning in her gaze. Whatever it was between them, chemistry or simple awareness, she felt something, too.

She backed up, putting one step and then another between them. Her gaze dropped to her hand, as she fidgeted with the doorknob of the door.

"Well then, goodnight." She closed the door behind her, leaving him on his own in the quiet.

Shelby was breathless as she backed away from the closed door. What had happened in there for those few brief moments?

She walked to the kitchen and took a glass down from the cupboard by the sink. Taking the pitcher from the refrigerator, she poured herself a glass of the lemonade without looking at what she was doing.

She stared out the window, watching the darkness fall heavier and heavier. In a few short minutes, the new boarder had managed to make her forget a lot of things. She had even forgotten that she was sad.

Her reverie was broken with the slam of the back door. Her uncle walked in, his face was dark, his skin a grayish mask, his shoulders hunched forward.

"What is it? What's wrong?" A familiar panic rose within her.

"I've been searching for your foolish brother."

"Did you find him? Is he okay?"

Her uncle's face softened at her words. His concern for her and her brother was something she had come to cherish since her father's death. He had become invaluable to her in her dealings with the store and the wharf, but there was still sometimes when even his company wasn't enough.

"He was down at the bar having a few with those friends of his. He said he would be along in a while."

Shelby let out the breath she'd been holding tight. The tension of the last few hours faded as he stepped into the light of the kitchen. He gave her a small reassuring smile. His usually light brogue became heavier with emotion and fatigue from a night of searching.

Shelby pulled out a kitchen chair and sank into it, thankful for the convenience.

"I know you worry about him, Shelby, but you can't protect him for the rest of his life. He's making foolish choices and he has no one to blame, but himself." He put a reassuring hand on her shoulder.

"Maybe, but I can't lose him. I can't lose another person in my life." She had already lost her parents and her husband. To lose Josh, too . . .

"I understand, but this is something Josh will have to find out for himself. He took it hard when your father died and he thinks he has to prove himself by making enough money to build himself a fancy boat. He just doesn't realize that he's going about it the wrong way."

"I know. I just wish there were something I could do for him. I want to help him, but you know yourself that the finances for the wharf and the store are shaky at best. I'm still paying off the loans. Maybe if we have another good summer next year then things will look better. But right now, I'm having a hard time competing with the other wharves for the dwindling business. There are just too many regulations. Too many of the locals are having a hard time just making a living."

He shook his head. "Right now, I'm more concerned about Josh's diving. Please promise me you'll try and talk to him again about giving it up? I think he'll listen to you. He shouldn't be out there by himself. The diving is dangerous enough, but the risk could be more than he expects." A shadow crossed his face as his words settled within her. He was right. Josh was in over his head and there wasn't a damn thing she could do about it.

"I'll try talking to him again, but I don't have too much effect on him."

"Yes, well, trying is better than doing nothing at all."

He let out a tired yawn as he pulled off

his boots and set them next to the back door. He straightened, stretching his back.

"I'd best be getting some sleep. It's been a long night and morning comes early." He started to pass by her in the cramped kitchen before he stopped. "I'll see you in the morning." He put his large hand upon her shoulder, giving her a reassuring squeeze. "Try not to worry about Josh. I'll make sure he'll be okay." He leaned over, kissing her forehead before turning to disappear down the darkened hallway.

It wasn't until she heard the soft click of his door shutting that she realized she had forgotten to talk to him about the latest addition to their household.

Jamie Rivard, with his teasing grin and mysterious scar, was sure to shake things up in Chandler.

She let out a yawn and reached over to switch off the light above the sink. Quietness settled around her as she moved through the house, shutting off the remaining lights as she went. She was just setting her own shoes out for the morning when the screech of the back door startled her.

Her brother flipped on the kitchen light and shrugged out of his jacket, hanging it by the back door. She could smell the faint stench of cigarettes, beer and bait on him.

His hair was tousled and deep, tired lines rimmed his eyes.

He headed for the refrigerator, pulling an apple out and taking a bite of it. The sound echoed through the still house.

"I was worried about you."

He stiffened at her words, but kept munching on the apple. She didn't want to get into another argument with him tonight, but there was a part of her that just couldn't help being scared by the chances he insisted on taking.

"We've had this discussion before, Sis. I'm not Tom and I'm not a little boy anymore. You need to let me live my own life and make my own mistakes. No matter what they are. You need to stop mothering me so much, Shel."

His quiet words stung her. She knew better than anyone that Josh wasn't Tommy. Still, he was her brother and he was the only brother she had.

"I know I worry too much." He gave a little snort as he bit into his apple again. "But I don't understand why you are taking so many chances. You don't know that much about diving. You could get in a bind, run out of air, or something could happen to the equipment and you would be all by yourself out there."

Josh tossed the apple core into the trashcan by the stove and turned to face her. His six-foot frame towered over her in the tiny, cramped kitchen. He had outgrown her by the time that he had turned sixteen. All the men in the Case family were tall and strong. All of them, driven by something.

She looked up at him and the anger and hurt in his eyes. It was too late, in too many ways. Most of all, it was too late to be having this conversation and it was too late to try to convince him that what he was doing was foolish. Josh had made up his own mind about the diving and she wasn't going to be able to change it with just a few words from an overprotective sister.

"If I had the money I would give it to you. I just don't have it right now." She reached out to put a hand on his arm. But he shouldered by her. He was mad at her and at life in general. And there wasn't anything she could do about it. The only thing she could do was hope for the best. He turned in the doorway to the living room and stared back at her.

"You don't have to worry about my diving for much longer. In a couple of days I'll have enough to build the boat, even some extra." He shook his head. "I told you I could do it. But you just couldn't believe in me. I'm going to have my boat built and it's going to be the best around. Then, you and everyone else won't have anything to talk about, anymore." He stalked off into the darkness of the living room, leaving her looking after him.

This wasn't a new argument. She knew how hard it was on him. When their father had died, she had inherited the store and wharf, and he had inherited their father's old lobster boat that was always in need of repairs. She could understand his hurt and his need to prove himself. What she couldn't understand was the anger behind it all.

He had all of his money for the boat now? That was a surprise. She knew he had been working hard. But even with the catch being as good as it had been, she couldn't see how he could have made enough. She let out another tired sigh and rolled her shoulders to ease the tension. She would have to talk with him about the money, later.

For now, she was restless. She was in need of a walk to calm her nerves and put some distance between her and the events of the night. She would take her usual route around the point in hopes that the night air would release the tension and fear that were threatened to engulf her, pulling her under.

She needed to escape.

Chapter Four

Jamie watched her skirt the darkened edges of the lawn, moving along the shoreline. Through the window in his room, he had a good view of the harbor and the moon glinting off the rippling edges of the water.

Where could she be going at this hour? It was late, much too late to be going out.

He hadn't meant to eavesdrop, but the quiet house had old walls with little insulation to muffle the raised voices of Shelby and her brother. Fate was lending him a helping hand by placing him in Shelby Teague's house. He would be able to keep an eye on her brother's activities and still scope out the area by going out on the boat with Case.

He watched her shadowy form disappear around the point. Shelby Teague was a grown woman, and from what he had seen and heard, she was fully capable of taking care of herself and everyone around her. He stretched out on the soft bed; his arms folded behind his head as he stared up at the silver gray spot the moonlight cast on the wall. The comfort of the quilt and the quiet house was lulling him into a soft security. But he couldn't afford to get too comfortable. He wouldn't be here for long.

He focused on the spot on the wall, as he concentrated on the facts at hand. The way that he figured, he was just where he should be. His list of people with possible ties to the smuggling activity had included Shelby's brother. Being in her home just made it all the easier to keep a watch on him. If he were in need of fast cash, then he would be an easy mark for someone who was trying to enlist a local to help move whatever merchandise they were transporting. Usually, it only took a flash of green in just the right direction to make someone question their long-held beliefs and morals — and trash them. He'd seen it too many times to count.

McAlvey was right; Shelby's wharf offered the perfect place for someone who wanted to smuggle something without calling too much attention to himself. Bait trucks and cold storage trailers were moving in and out of that area daily. What was one more truck? And no one would be the wiser. He made a mental note to keep an eye on the traffic in the area of the wharf.

He got up from the bed and went to the door, swinging it open an inch or two until he had a clear view of the hallway and part of the dining room. No one in sight. He stepped out into the hall and made his way toward the kitchen, all the while listening for any kind of noise that would alert him that others were about. Through the floor above he heard the heavy footfall of Shelby's brother and the creak of bedsprings. He must be settling in for the night.

He let himself out the back door, taking care not to let it bang, and picked his way across the lawn. If anyone did spot him he would just tell them he was restless, but what he was really looking for was a safe place to make a phone call.

He followed the same path he had seen Shelby take down to the water. Here the lawn dipped toward the ledges and green grass became rocks and seaweed. He settled himself on an oversized rock and sat still for a moment, listening. It was so very quiet here. No traffic noises, no hum of civilization with only the sound of the water coming ashore.

He pulled his cell phone out of his pocket and punched out a number, waiting until he heard the sleepy response on the other end.

"Damn it, Rivard! You never did hear of calling at a decent hour. I'm on my first time off in thirty-six hours and the next thing I know I have to get out of bed to listen to you ramble on about how you got your sorry butt into a mess."

Jamie let out a chuckle. "Nice to hear your sweet voice again, too, Kearsage."

"I suppose you need me to bail you out? What did you do this time? Let that sweet-talking talent of yours land you on the wrong side of some lady's husband?"

"Nothing that mild. I need help with something going on in your own backyard." He could hear shuffling on the other end. Sounded like he had managed to get Kearsage wide-awake now.

"You bastard. You're in Maine and you didn't even let me know you were coming?"

"As far as you or anyone else is concerned, I am not in Maine. Got it?"

"Okay, okay. Got it. The way I figure, I still owe you a few for bailing my butt out on that overblown investigation two years ago. So, what do you need?"

"I need to know what you have on two known traffickers that are sitting on an island off of Chandler. I need to know how far the investigation has gone."

There was silence on the other end for a long moment. "Man, what have you gotten yourself into this time, Rivard? I haven't a clue what you're talking about. The only thing we have going on near there is that we are watching for two known Miami operatives named Caruso and Taimon. But if they're around they're keeping a low profile." Gone was the sarcastic flip in his voice, replaced with a quiet undercurrent of tension.

"You mean that you can't tell me what is going on. I understand. I'll handle it on my own here." The last thing that he wanted to do was get Kearsage nailed for giving out classified information. He would have to handle it on his own. He owed him that much. Kearsage had done his own fair share of bailing him out a time or two.

"I wish that I could tell you something, but I can't." Again, he hesitated. "If something changes I'll let you know."

"I'd appreciate it." Kearsage's lack of information didn't settle too well with him. He trusted him enough to know that unless it was something huge, he wouldn't let him walk into it without enough information to cover him. But it appeared that Kearsage either didn't know what was going on or he was under orders not to say. Either way it didn't look very good for him.

He hung up the phone, feeling more confused than he had before he had called. He had way too few answers to the questions at hand. He rubbed at the piercing sensation that was climbing up his neck and numbing his brain.

So they were looking for two known Miami operatives in Casco Bay? What were the chances of them being here when he was looking for a connection with David's investigation? That was just too big of a what-if for him . . .

And he had heard enough about Caruso and Taimon to know that they had ties to any number of smuggling operations on all along the Atlantic seaboard with varying loyalties. Caruso was the brain of the two; smart enough to carry out the details, but not quite smart enough to set them all up. Taimon was the brawn. What he lacked in logical thinking, he made up for in sheer size.

Neither of them were the friendly types. They had a history of trafficking in anything from artifacts to drugs and they especially didn't like it when someone got in their way. If Taimon and Caruso had ventured this far north, then they had to have a very good reason for being here. They were more the warm weather types, sharks who were used to the Keys' balmy waters and the hidden outlaw mentality that made it easy for them to disappear when need be.

Aside from those two, all he had to go on were unconfirmed reports of large amounts of money surfacing in the Chandler area within the last six months. Whatever it was that they were moving, it was most likely being transported by boat to the harbor and then moved inland for distribution.

Still, he had no hard information on how the drops were being made and transported. They could have been coming in by seagull for all he knew. He was flying blind here. He had less to go on than those TV detectives who were able to solve a crime in thirty minutes.

He didn't know who or what or even where or when. All of the information he had were unconfirmed reports and the speculation McAlvey had given him from an unreliable source, a petty criminal who was being held on burglary charges in the Cumberland County Jail in Portland.

He had nothing to go on except for the discussion he had just overheard and Kearsage's reluctance to talk. He had solved cases with less.

His preliminary information had told him very little about what to expect, but sudden money in a small town usually meant something big was going on. He would hate to suspect that Shelby's brother was behind it, but, for now, however, he couldn't rule out anyone or anything. At least not until he had more information.

He slipped the cell phone back onto his waistband and got up, his muscles aching from the hard seat. He headed back across the lawn toward the house. Shelby Teague had been an interesting surprise. He liked surprises.

What he hadn't counted on was how the simple curve of her arm or the touch of her hand in his had sent warning flares shooting through him. Too bad she was off limits.

Every piece of the puzzle that he had managed to acquire said that Shelby was also a possible suspect. At least until proven otherwise. He had to admit, though, she was convincing as a widow struggling to make a business go in an unpredictable market — a woman protective of her brother who was knee deep in his own motives and debt — with an uncle who was hiding his own secrets. There was bound to be endless scars under her cover. Even if he did find her interesting, he wasn't willing to complicate it all by giving in to a passing attraction, just for the hell of it. There was too much at stake. There was too much to lose for both of them.

Even if all she was hiding was a hurtful past, he couldn't be the one to help her deal with it. He had his own past that he was fighting. And he needed to stay focused, for David's sake.

He slipped through the back door and down the hall, letting himself back into his room. His last words to McAlvey echoed in his brain. McAlvey could be damned certain that he would see him again once this was through. He wasn't going to allow himself to be railroaded into giving up on finding out what had happened to David. If there was a connection between this case and the one that David had been working on when he died, then Jamie was going to do his damnedest to find out what that connection was.

But there was something about this whole case that raised the hairs on his neck. He wasn't one to get spooked easily, but this was just too strange, even for him. He had too many personal connections to the case. There was David's death and McAlvey's guarded request that he be the one to take it on even though he was on medical leave.

And then there was his connection to Maine.

It wasn't a secret. He just wasn't in the habit of dragging up old painful memories. But if McAlvey had sent him here because of his connection to Maine, then maybe he knew the real reason why he hadn't been back in years. And if McAlvey did know about his past, then that was yet another unsolved piece to this puzzle.

He lay down on the quilt, running his hand along the crevice where the blanket met the pillow, checking for the 9mm gun he'd placed beneath his pillow. The chances of his needing it were slim — probably not at all — but it was always best to be prepared. He yawned as the events of the day caught up with him. His leg throbbed again, reminding him that it was not yet completely healed. The doctors had said that it would be some time before the effects of the injury went away altogether. He propped the leg up on an extra pillow that he had found in the top of the closet and settled in. He had to get some rest.

He had a lot to do in the morning and the first thing was to get himself some new boots.

Caruso watched the lights in the distance

coming on one by one in Chandler's nestled little harbor.

The phone rang under the muffled confines of his coat. Caruso flipped the receiver and punched the button before holding it up to his ear.

"Yeah?"

"Rivard should be there. You know what to do?" Caruso recognized the old man's voice.

"Yes, but why don't —"

"I want him taken care of as soon as possible and as quietly as possible. Do you understand?"

"Why don't we just set him up? Let him take the blame and let the authorities catch him and deal with him? It'll give us time to get away and no one will know a thing."

The voice on the other end of the line was silent for a long moment.

"No, I want it done as planned. Do not change course. I want him gone, but I don't want to make anyone more suspicious than they already are and risk having him figure out what is going on. When this is done Jamie Rivard will find himself a casualty of a nasty accident."

"Understood. We'll take care of it for you. No problem."

"See to it," the old man said.

The line went dead leaving Caruso with the receiver buzzing in his ear. He punched the button to end the call and then stuffed the phone back in his pocket. They were all set now. They knew what they had to do. And there would be no mistakes.

Like the night before, the sky was deep black with little moon to light the way. She had been here so many times she could have walked the path in her sleep. But even with her familiarity she was unsettled by the cloak of night surrounding her.

The air was warm and fragrant. All around her the rich smell of juniper lent sweetness to the air. The gravel crunched beneath her feet as she walked down the twin-rutted lanes of the narrow dirt road. The normal chirp of the birds was absent, giving it an even eerier feel.

As she got closer to the beach she could hear the sound of the waves washing to shore. The rhythmic in and out of the water made her more at ease and she found herself thinking of the new boarder.

Jamie Rivard.

There was something about the man that was different than any other she'd met. His manners and voice held the strains of southern genteel while his style of dress and transportation was more on the wild side. He was a contradiction.

How he had managed to get her uncle to hire him was beyond her. People around here were known for distrusting outsiders. But then, her uncle knew that as well as any other. She tended to forget that it wasn't that long ago that her uncle had come to Chandler to help after her father's death.

In the darkness in front of her, she could picture him. She let out a soft chuckle. She considered herself a good judge of character, but he didn't fit any stereotype that she had ever seen. He was friendly, yet standoffish. He had a swaggering confidence that he countered with a boyish charm.

And then there was the question of the limp. The slight hesitation wasn't noticeable during their first meeting, but she had watched him through the kitchen window when he arrived at the house. She had seen the hitch in his stride, the uneasy moment of hesitation when he stood up. He disguised his discomfort well, but she had seen enough to know that something about his leg wasn't right. Maybe it was tied to the scar. It was a new scar, still raised and discolored. Whatever had happened to him, hadn't happened very long ago.

She didn't consider herself naïve. She had

gone to college and had other relationships before her marriage, but there was something about the way he looked at her that made her feel like she was someone different. She wasn't looking for romance. But it would be nice to have someone new and interesting around for as long as it lasted. Somewhere beneath that cocky exterior was a man who she might like to meet. She just wasn't sure how to find him.

Her feet hit soft sand and she trudged on, sinking into the loose coarse earth. She walked closer to the shoreline until she came to the point where the ledges stuck out into the ocean.

Shelby searched out the hand- and footholds that she knew by heart and lifted herself up. A breeze was kicking up off the water brushing against her skin.

She settled herself in her usual spot, well away from the waves and high up on the ledges, and waited. There were no boats, no planes tonight, nothing but the wind to make a noise.

After twenty minutes, the slight wind had managed to put a chill into her and clouds were moving in fast making the sheltered cove even darker. It must have been coincidence that she had seen the plane last night, a trick of the wind that she had thought she had seen something drop.

She was a fool to think that something strange and suspicious was happening in Chandler. Nothing ever happened here. With a sigh, Shelby began gathering herself together and readying to once again make the trek back home. A good night's sleep would help her forget her troubles with her brother.

Her dark mood returned as she thought about Josh. The look on her uncle's face, when he had returned from hunting for her brother, had been enough to scare her all over again. Josh's disappearance had once again brought up all the feelings that Tommy's death had caused. All the feelings of helplessness that she'd gone through when he had disappeared came crashing back upon her. What had happened to Tommy had been an accident, a twist of fate that he'd brought on himself. The thing that she understood that Josh didn't was that, as senseless and random as it was, it could easily happen again. Only this time it could happen to Josh.

Shelby started picking her way back down the ledge, straining her eyes in the dark as she sought out hand- and footholds in the rock. And then she heard the sound again.

The wind was calmer this time. The sound

grew clearer from farther away; giving her time to watch for the plane that she knew was coming.

Shelby crouched down, stuck in a crevice of rocks as she listened to the sound of the plane drawing closer.

It was approaching low and from the east, just as it had before. Darkness prevented her from making out any of the markings, only the small marker lights and the shadowy outline of large landing pontoons.

The plane moved low over the cove before making a sharp turn and heading back again over the open water. If this was some sort of a pattern she wanted to make sure that she watched everything, taking in every note, every detail. A shiver ran through her. She hadn't been imagining it the other night — there really had been something out there.

The sound of the engines echoing off the rocks deafened her, even as she strained to hear above it, listening for a splash. The plane circled low again and then headed back out over the water, hugging the edge of the shoreline.

As the sound of the plane died out, she crept down from her place among the rocks. Whatever was going on was a mystery. She should tell someone about what she was seeing. But just what was it that she had seen? Was it nothing more than some idiot out on a dark night practicing his night flying? Or was something much more dangerous going on in Chandler?

The next morning, Shelby was still mulling over what she had seen. Just this morning Roe and John Henry had been grumbling about strange happenings, but she had discounted it as their own eccentric ramblings. As with everything that happened in Chandler, there wasn't a soul who didn't have an opinion on the odd comings and goings. Up until now, she had just credited it to the substantial gossip network that ran through the harbor. Small things had a tendency to get bigger and bigger, as stories were told and soon things became monumental. She had never been one to pay much attention to what was being pushed about, but maybe there was something to it this time.

Maybe she should mention the plane sighting to someone, but to whom? The sheriff? He would only suggest that she needed to get more sleep and stay off the point in the dark. She could mention it to her uncle. But right now he was too busy chasing after Josh and his antics, to worry about her late night sightings. No, she would keep her mouth shut and her eyes open. If it happened again, then she would tell someone.

She pushed at the ancient keys of the old manual cash register, totaling up the order that Marianne had asked her to drop off. The elderly, arthritic artist lived in a large home out on the point with only her cat for company. Shelby looked after her, delivering groceries or running errands for the homebound lady. Marianne had enough money to hire someone to look after her, but she had lived alone for so long that she now refused to call upon anyone else.

Shelby looked up from the pile of cat food that she was ringing up, in time to see her boarder come striding into the store. He waved a hand in greeting and gave her one of those small grins that set her heart beating faster.

All morning long, she had tried hard to convince herself that her interest in Jamie Rivard was simple curiosity. It was her imagination at its best. But now, seeing him standing there larger than life, in the close confines of the cluttered store, she wasn't quite sure that it was curiosity after all.

"Good morning. I trust that you slept well?" She forced a smile and leveled what she hoped was a polite, but disinterested look in his direction. It was a mistake. He wasn't wearing the sunglasses today and as he walked toward her with his easy long gait, she was able to get a close-up look at his eyes. They were the color of a graying ocean tide with a storm coming, fierce, ominous and powerful.

She had to concentrate to keep her mouth from hanging open and embarrassing her. When she began seeing dating possibilities in her boarders it was a sure sign that she'd been avoiding life for too long. Why the next thing she knew she would be after Roe and John Henry and both of those old fishermen were in their eighties.

"I missed you this morning. You were already up and gone by the time that I got up."

The tone was intimate, much more so than she was comfortable with. Thank goodness, there wasn't anyone else in the store this morning to overhear. Even if his words were just casual, with the town's gossip network, she would be a branded woman by nightfall. Within a couple of days, they would have them engaged and on their way to the altar and all without leaving the confines of their own snug little houses.

"You must get up pretty early to get here

and get everything done. It has to be a big job all by yourself."

His voice was a mix of husky caress and a yawning purr. This man could give the maritime broadcast and make it sound sexy with his slow southern drawl. She placed a few more items on the counter and checked her list.

"I always leave before dawn so that I can get everything done before the wharf business picks up in the afternoon. A lot of my business happens before the sun is up." She finished ringing up the other items and placed them in the bag with the other stuff. Then she placed the bags in a blue plastic box.

Like an idiot, she was doing everything in her power to avoid looking in his face again. It was an unnerving feeling, being attracted to someone, and something that she hadn't felt in a very long time. She wasn't used to the heated feelings that came with the unfamiliar territory and she couldn't remember the last time she had felt so out of sorts.

He walked around the small store, examining things and picking up items here and there. She was being foolish, but she just didn't know what else to do. She was a capable and responsible woman, a widow, for goodness sake, with two businesses to run. She didn't have time to be mooning over a man she'd just met.

"I was just wondering when it is that you do sleep?"

Her heart fluttered at the breathless quality of his voice. He was inspecting a small seagull miniature that was glued to a piece of driftwood, a tourist trinket.

"Are you keeping tabs on me, Mr. Rivard? I don't think that my sleep patterns are of much concern to you." Now that sounded huffy. She grimaced a little and fidgeted with the bags and items in the box. She was beginning to sound like some crazy old lady.

Setting the last of the items into the plastic box, Shelby was preparing to pick it up when Jamie reached down and lifted the box by the handles onto the edge of the counter. But not before she saw the slightest falter in his movements.

The hesitation had been small. A slight wince, an unsteady hitch in his rise. She had been right to suspect that he had some sort of injury. Whatever it was, it appeared that he didn't want to call attention to it.

"I notice a lot of things about you. Including the late night walk that you took last night. It must have been a nice night to be out. Maybe you'll allow me to come with you sometime."

He had seen her leave? She dared a look at his face and saw the twinkle of amusement in his eyes. She looked away, embarrassed as a schoolgirl. What was it about this man that made her alternate between irritation and attraction?

"I don't think you would like walking with me, Mr. Rivard. I take a very brisk walk around the point to clear my head and help me sleep. I don't take the time to do much sightseeing." Most of the time there isn't much to see, she added to herself. But the last few nights had changed her opinion on that matter. She had witnessed enough in the last couple of nights to keep her sleepless for a while. "I'm guessing that you won't be around long enough to be going on any walks with me."

He just smiled at her. "Maybe. Maybe not."

The man was a master of saying the most, with a minimal amount of words. "Just how long are you going to be here, Mr. Rivard?"

He shrugged, pushing away from his spot against the counter. His eyebrows drew together in concentration and his smile thinned to a straight line. "I don't know. I'll let you know when I figure it out. Unless, of course, you're concerned that I'm going to skip out of the rent."

"No, I think you can be trusted . . . to pay the rent, that is."

Her small hesitation was enough to emit a small laugh from him. "I assure you. I can be trusted."

She grasped the handles of the box and hoisted it off the counter. Using her legs to offset the weight of the box, she headed in the direction of the door. Within seconds, her arms ached from the pull of the box and she regretted not paying more attention to what she'd put in. But then, she hadn't counted on being distracted. Still, she wasn't about to let him know that the added weight bothered her. She'd spent most of her adult life trying to convince people that she could handle dealing in a man's world. A lot of people grumbled when she took over the store and the wharf, and there were many who had said that she wouldn't be able to do it for very long. She'd shown them that she could handle it all — and she wasn't about to back down now.

She was almost to the door before her conscience began nagging. Jamie may be a stranger, but she was raised to be polite. Balancing the box against a shelf by the door, Shelby turned, expecting to find him standing by the counter and found herself facing an expanse of white cotton fabric, stretched taught across broad shoulders. They were very nice shoulders. The box started to slide from her hands and she grabbed for it, her fingers fumbling against his as he reached out to help her. The last thing she needed was to have him think that she couldn't handle a simple box.

"Sorry, I didn't mean to startle you. I was just going to get the door for you since you had such a load." He stepped around her, opening the door and levering his back against it to hold it open. "Here, I can take that for you. It looks heavy."

But Shelby just shook her head as she struggled to hoist the box up to a comfortable level. She was having trouble getting her fingers to do what she wanted them to do and getting her brain to form acceptable sentences. He smelled good; a musky smell that didn't overpower, only lingered about to remind.

"That's all right, I've got it," she grumbled, her words sounding rough even to her own ears. "I just didn't realize that you were behind me, that's all. You could scare a person half to death sneaking up on them like that." Just standing this close to him had an unnerving effect on her. Jamie held open the door wide for her as she stepped out onto the granite steps. She had been cooped up in this store for too long. Her manners were rusty and he was, after all, only being polite.

"It's a beautiful day out. Do you mind if I help you deliver that? I have some time this morning since I'm not going out on the boat with your uncle until tomorrow." He reached his hands out to take the box from her. "I could use the exercise and I would kind of like to get a feel for the area, figure out where everything is."

"I'm not going far. I'm just taking this out to a lady that lives on the point."

He stood in front of her, hands on hips, squinting at her in the sunlight. "Consider this an olive branch, an apology for the way I acted the other day. Besides, that looks pretty heavy." He smiled at her. "Not that I don't have total confidence that you can handle it."

Maybe he was trying to make amends. "I guess this is heavier than I thought. If you want to help me take it out to her then I'll treat you to lunch." She must be a fool. He had offered help and she had offered him lunch. The last thing that she needed was to have him thinking that she was making advances toward him.

"That's great. I'm starving." As if it were

the easiest thing in the world, Jamie took the box from her and strode toward the truck, hoisting it over the back of the truck body and setting it behind the cab. Shelby followed him to the truck. It was just an offer of help. Nothing more, certainly nothing to be worried about. Shelby reached for the door handle, but Jamie's hand had already closed over the latch. He pulled open the truck's door for her, ushering her in, closing it behind her. All of this courtesy could go to her head.

Jamie crossed to his side of the truck and got in, slamming the door behind him.

"Sorry about the mess. I don't get much time to clean up the old truck." She watched him roll down the window and settle his arm on the door as though it was the most common thing in the world.

"Don't worry. I'll survive. Besides it isn't every day that I get to have a pretty lady chauffeur me around." Heat braced cheeks as he flashed a heart-stopping grin flash her way. It may have been a long time since he'd had a chauffeur, but it was even longer since she had gotten a compliment.

The trip to the point was made in relative silence. The only sound was the static filled conversation of the fishermen on the dash-mounted radio. The sun was warm, sparkling off the green, red and gold of the leaves rustling in the morning breeze. The dirt road to the point was a maze of ruts, covered at times by the canopy of trees that clustered next to the road. Shelby maneuvered the truck around the majority of holes that were big enough to engulf the truck. It was like stepping into a private retreat with no one else there, except for them.

"Your friend lives out here alone? It's rather remote, isn't it?" He placed an arm on the window to brace himself for another bump.

"Maybe, she likes it that way. I should warn you before we get there that Marianne is a rather unique lady. She's an artist." She navigated the truck around another pothole. "And she's quite successful, but you'd never know it to talk to her. She prefers to live out here alone rather than be around a lot of people." She pulled the truck into a driveway hidden among a bank of beach roses.

"Have you known her a long time?"

"Since I was a little girl. After my mom died I would get lonely and she would let me come and watch her paint." She stopped the truck at the gate and Jamie jumped out to swing it open before climbing back into the truck.

The gravel road gave way to a paved driveway. The house was barely visible from the road.

Late summer flowers bloomed among the masses of white, purple and pink hydrangea bushes lining the driveway. A green lawn dotted with bright blossoms swept downward to a weathered gray cape perched on the ledges overlooking the water. A simple white porch ran along the back and sides of the house and was screened in to keep the bugs out.

Shelby pulled the truck up next to an aging Volvo and cut the ignition. Jamie jumped out and pulled the box out of the back of the truck, following her toward the porch.

Her booted feet scuffed on the dirt walkway. He watched the sway of her hips over the top of his load. She was wearing those faded denims again, the ones that hugged to her long, slim legs. This time there was no oversized shirt to obstruct his view. Instead, she was wearing a pink polo shirt with the words Chandler stitched in blue on it. The fabric was wash worn and rode up a little as she walked. She had a very nice walk. It wasn't a wiggle, more of an educated sway. She was a woman who walked with confidence, easily eating up the distance to the house and giving him a great chance to observe her.

Which was exactly the reason why he was having a hard time remembering that Shelby was not his type. He preferred to stick with women who loved to have a good time and then move on. He'd always been careful to look for women who were no more interested in a commitment than he was.

Shelby Teague was a staying kind of woman. She was a remarkable woman, self-confident, determined, and able to handle anything and do it well. Damn, she was beautiful. But the thing that made her so beautiful was that she was unaware of how pretty she really was. Shelby Teague was a dangerous advisory. Too bad she wasn't his type.

Jamie waited while Shelby knocked on the door.

"Use the key. I'm working," came the muffled reply. Shelby pulled a key off the chain she had around her neck, fit it into the lock and opened the door.

He followed through a small mudroom and into a bright sunny kitchen with high white cabinets and a big window that looked out over the lawn. The walls were painted a brilliant turquoise color, and the room was simply furnished with a small table and chairs. But the thing that surprised him most was that everywhere he looked there was something with a cat on it. Jamie set the box on the counter. There were mugs and plates, placemats, even curtains at the window, and every last one of them had cats on them.

An orange tabby came in and wound herself around his legs, rubbing its face against her jeans. Jamie reached down to scratch her under the chin and it sat back on its haunches, a loud purr growling from it in pure pleasure.

Shelby laughed. "Meribelle, you old reprobate. You just love a good scratch, don't you? You just know that I brought your food for you?"

Meribelle abandoned Jamie to twine around Shelby's feet and then rolled onto her back for a belly rub.

"It looks like you've got quite a friend there."

Shelby reached down to give one last scratch. "Meribelle isn't too partial. She'll go to anyone who is willing to give her a scratch. Besides, she's only loyal to me because she knows that I bring her food. Of course she's going to like me."

"Shelby, is that you?" The voice was coming from somewhere near the front of the house.

"It's just me," Shelby yelled. "I brought over those groceries you wanted. I was just about to put them away for you, but Meribelle decided that I would make a better resting spot instead."

There was a jingle of bracelets and the scuffle of footsteps coming down the hall long before she appeared in the doorway. Marianne's gray-white hair hung long past her shoulders and was tinted with a purple rinse that made her look like a cross between a punk rocker and an Easter egg. She wore an orange paint-speckled shirt with a pair of loose fitting blue-green chef style pants the color of deep, ocean water. Purple canvas high-top sneakers completed her outfit.

"Oh good. I see you brought a friend with you." She held her hand out to him. Her long fingers were adorned with many rings and her wrists jangled with rows of silver bracelets. Her fingers rested against his hand for a moment before she looked over at Shelby and winked. "It's about time that you brought someone with you."

Not waiting for a response, Marianne angled herself past him and over to the stove to put the teakettle on to heat. Her movements were stilted with the effects of arthritis, but even with the restrictions, she carried herself with an air of elegant grace.

"You'll stay to tea. I can't let you go without, since you were nice enough to bring all that out here." She motioned toward the counter. "Goodness gracious, Shelby. You should have made more than one trip. You shouldn't be hauling all of that over in one load."

"It's not really that heavy. Besides I brought help to carry it." Shelby walked over to the counter next to him and began pulling cat food from the bags and placing the cans in the cupboard next to the sink.

The cat let out a disgruntled yowl at Jamie as he pulled his foot out from under its lounging body and Marianne looked at him over half-glasses perched on her nose. "So do you have a name or did she pick you up on the side of the road?"

"My name is Jamie Rivard." He was surprised when she took his hand in hers again and looked into his eyes. He had the strange feeling that he was somehow being analyzed.

Marianne turned back to Shelby who was now putting the cold items into the refrigerator. "He's okay. You can bring him back again, dear." Shelby didn't look up from her task, but Jamie could see her face was turning red in the light from the refrigerator.

"How is the painting today? Making any progress?" Shelby asked.

"Oh, not much, I'm afraid." She scuffed her purple sneakers over to the counter. Marianne gave a sad shake of her head as she pulled down three worn coffee mugs and motioned to him. "I was going to try this wonderful green tea blend that I picked up at a small shop in New York. I can't say a lot for the flavor, but it's supposed to be good for me, so I drink it anyway." The teakettle started to whistle so she pulled it from the burner and filled the mugs with hot water. She handed a cup to him and one to Shelby and then headed toward the doorway, leading to the rest of the house. She motioned them to follow with the tinkling of her bracelets.

"Shelby, I wish you would take a look at this piece I'm working on. I could use another person's perspective on this blasted thing and you have a good eye for it. Something just isn't right and I was up most of last night just staring at it trying to figure it out."

Jamie followed them down a narrow hallway that opened into a sunlit room. Wide

French doors opened up onto a large deck that faced the ocean below. A gentle breeze swept the room, ruffling papers on a large drawing board that sat in one corner. The room was filled with comfortable pieces, a floral covered couched and an overstuffed chair. There was a certain ease here, a quiet elegance and easy styling, much like many of the traditional old Maine cottages along the coast.

A white wicker chair had been pulled up to an old wooden drawing board. A set of watercolors held one edge of a large painting in place. He looked at the softened colors that filled the page with subtle strength and beauty. The painting was incredible. Marianne had managed to capture the tiniest details with the sweep of her brush. She had transferred the world outside her window onto the paper. Her simplistic style captured the very essence of a graying mist that filled the small harbor in the morning. The water reflected a boat, as it made its way out to haul. The white of the boat's hull was in stark contrast to the deepness of the surrounding water. The green of the pine trees lining the bank and the stark black and grays of the rocks looked real enough to touch and the small islands dotting the entrance to the harbor were like ghosts of gray silhouette in the background.

"I can't imagine that there is anything wrong with this picture. It's the most beautiful piece that you've done." Shelby assured her as she stood next to her in front of the easel.

"Oh, well, thank you. Not bad for these old bones, is it?" She picked up the picture and carried it to the window to compare it to the scene beyond the glass. "I think that I got the rocks along the edge of the embankment here just right." She pointed at the picture and then out the window, tracing an invisible line along the edge of the rocks where the grass of the lawn ended and the craggy shore began. It was an abrupt drop to the ocean, the trail of ledges leading down to the dock, about twenty feet below. A small Boston Whaler was tied at the dock, bobbing in the wake of the boats that passed on their way in and out of the harbor.

Jamie watched as Shelby drifted toward the window and picked up the binoculars on the windowsill. Sunlight glinted off the dark and light tones of her hair as she raised the binoculars to her face. Out in the harbor a boat passed by. He didn't need the binoculars to know that the markings showed that it was a local boat.

"There's been quite a bit going on out

there as of late. It's enough to keep a nosy old woman, like me, quite busy." Marianne said, as she fidgeted with putting the painting back onto the easel.

"More than usual?" Shelby said.

He watched a startled expression cross Shelby's face.

"Oh, goodness, there has been all kinds of activity going on out there, at all times of the day and night."

Shelby glanced in his direction. Her gaze met his and a moment of startled confusion crossed her features.

"You didn't happen to see anything last night did you? Say around ten?"

Marianne set her paints back onto the tray and looked out the window at the ocean. "I think I was up around that time last night, but I don't remember anything out of the ordinary."

The older lady shrugged as she passed by Shelby and headed toward the kitchen. "I've been watching the boats coming and going all summer. There's still a lot of water traffic in the area. It's a might weird having so many outsiders here, seeing how it's after Labor Day. Why, I think I'm the last one left out here on the point, now. Everyone else has closed up for the winter except for those two who have been using the neighbors' wharf while they're gone."

Marianne shuffled her purple sneakers off toward the kitchen and Shelby followed her, keeping her head down and avoiding his eyes. She knew something all right and she didn't want anyone else to know.

This put him in an awkward position. Shelby was the last person he wanted to suspect, but her reaction said differently. He had almost decided to take her off his list of suspects, but now he wasn't so sure. After all, she ran the two most public places in the little town and she knew more about all the comings and going of the harbor than anyone else. Owning the wharf and the store gave her a perfect opportunity to be involved in any trafficking that was going in and out of Chandler.

But as for motive, he didn't have a clue. From what he had observed, she wasn't a woman impressed with money. And she certainly wasn't the type to be doing it for personal gain. So once again he had more questions than answers.

On the other hand, if she wasn't involved, she might have stumbled onto what was going on here. That could put Shelby in danger and that was one thing Jamie didn't want to risk.

Chapter Five

They returned to the store in much the same way that they had gone, in silence. Shelby's mood had changed from one of quiet complacency to one of introspection. She was thinking hard about something and he would love to know what it was.

The bell above the store's door jingled, announcing their return. Case looked up from behind the counter and straightened a little, when he saw that Jamie was with Shelby. John Case was an imposing man. His thick cut shoulders resembled tree trunks and he had a sense about him that made him appear older than he really was.

Shelby did little more than give a muffled hello before disappearing into the back room leaving him and Case alone out front.

"Did she take you with her to Marianne's?" Case eyed him, over the display of canned goods.

"I offered to help her with the load." His

words sounded inane to his own ears. But what else could he say? He couldn't risk alienating Case. Going out on the boat with Case gave him a perfect opportunity to get a look at what was happening out in the harbor. Besides, he was still trying to figure out in his own mind just what had happened at Marianne's.

"I understand that Shelby gave you a place to stay. You must've passed muster, for her to let you in."

"She said the same thing about you when I told her you had offered me a job." He met Case's gaze for a moment before the other man turned away. Jamie knew when he was being sized up. It didn't take a genius to know that Case suspected that there was more going on between Shelby and him. The truth of the matter was that he wasn't sure himself.

Case poured himself a cup of black coffee from the pot on the counter, and settled back with his mug, into the chair by the window. He wore a smug smile. Jamie wasn't sure if he should run like hell or stick around to see what was on Case's mind.

"I help Shelby out around here and give her a hand when she needs one, which isn't often. The girl is more than capable of taking care of herself." The warning in his words was clear.

Case's gaze narrowed as he looked at him.

Jamie stared back. "From what I have seen, Shelby is more than capable of taking care of herself."

Case's hand stilled with the mug halfway to his mouth. "You are right. Shelby is not naïve, but she has a big heart. And sometimes people think that they can take advantage of it." Case set his mug on the counter and came around, slapping Jamie good-naturedly on the shoulder. "I'm glad that we understand each other. So what can I help you with today?"

Jamie was caught off balance by the sudden change in topic. He spotted the boots on a far shelf. They were lined up by size from the smallest to the largest, all the same navy-black color and all the same style like small little soldiers all in a row. So much for making a personal statement.

"I guess I had better get those boots I need." Both men looked down at his size-eleven feet at the same time.

"Let's see if we can find some in your size." By the time they had finished, Jamie had acquired a new pair of shiny, black rubber boots, a pair of thick rubber gloves to protect his hands and a pair of bright yellow coveralls. Hauling traps was hard dirty work and he would need the gear to do the work. They had fallen into a sort of companionable small talk. Saying a few things, but not much of anything at all.

"Your accent is Irish, isn't it?"

The older man nodded. "I grew up in Belfast and came to America after my brother died. My mother died when I was a teenager and my brother was quite a bit older than I was so he helped my father raise me. I guess I never did quite lose the accent all together." Case handed Jamie his gear over the counter.

"My brother was a writer. When I was old enough to take care of myself, he began traveling all over the world. Then, when he met his wife, he knew that he wanted to start a life here in Maine with her. They started this business on their own, running it themselves, until his wife died of cancer. After that, he managed to keep it all going and raise two kids on his own."

"It couldn't have been easy for him."

"No, but he realized that this was the best place for him to raise his children. We'd grown up seeing too much violence for him to want that for his kids. And he didn't want to be spending too much time away from Shelby and Josh. Running this place meant that he could be here for them." He shrugged.

"After he died I came to help Shelby out and I just kind of stayed. Shelby has seen too much loss in her life. I would hate to see her hurt more." The message was received and clear. Shelby Teague was off limits for a guy like him.

"Have you always been a fisherman?"

Case didn't look up from where he was putting boxes away. He hesitated for a moment before answering. "No, I did a stint in the Royal Navy and then I spent a lot of time doing a lot of different things. That's when I lost track of my brother." Case gave a shrug of his wide shoulders. "I didn't find out about his wife's death until long after it had happened."

Case turned, putting his coffee cup on the stand behind the counter. There was much more to what Case had said, than what he was letting on. His information was sketchy on Case, but it was enough to know that this man was as far from a mild-mannered fisherman as a person could get.

It would be best to keep him on his side if at all possible. He had other leads to look into and right now his first priority was to find out how Josh was planning on making his money for that boat.

"I was hoping to meet Josh this morning.

I guess I just missed him." He watched a shadow of concern cross Case's face before it disappeared.

"Josh left early this morning to go out hauling. I suspect that you'll meet him this evening at dinner. That is if the boy can manage to get himself back in early enough."

Jamie let it go. He didn't want to press anymore and risk arousing Case's suspicion. He suspected that he had won a grudging temporary acceptance from the man and he wasn't about to screw up his chances and blow his cover by asking too many questions at once. He would just have to seek another route to get the information that he needed.

The twenty-four-foot Bayliner, anchored in the sheltered cove of the pine-covered island, was small enough not to encourage unwanted attention. The island's large summer cottage was a definite advantage for their cover. To anyone who may take notice they looked like nothing more than a couple of late-season fishermen out trying their hand at catching bluefish, or the like.

As near as they could tell, no one had noticed the small raft buried under the dense brush cover surrounding the cove or the occasional switch of men who sat aboard the Florida-registered fishing boat.

Just one more week and the last shipment would be complete. After they had made the last exchange they could sink the boat and get rid of all the other signs that they had been using the island. They had one more drop to pick up and one more transfer and they would be home free.

It was his shift to keep guard. With such a small but important operation, everyone had to take a turn. So far, they had escaped the attention of the locals and had even bargained for a couple of lobsters from one of the boats fishing nearby. He pushed his sunglasses further up his nose and squinted out over the water. There wasn't much around this godforsaken place, just a hundred and eighty or so islands in which they could get lost while they did their business.

The beep of his cell phone caught his attention. He flipped it open and punched the button to connect.

"It's a go," the old man said.

This was the call they had been waiting for. "Okay on this end," Caruso answered.

"He's already in your area. You owe me this one. Don't let me down."

Caruso stifled a sigh. He wasn't about to forget how much they owed the old man.

"We can handle it," Caruso said.

"Good. Just make it so that he isn't a problem anymore."

"Understood. Just remember that after that job you did for us in the Keys this makes us even. What you are asking isn't small. He could be extra trouble." And the last thing they needed to worry about was a body turning up.

"Don't worry about the trouble," the old man said. "I'll take care of it. I have so far, haven't I? Just do as I ask."

The line went dead without the need for response.

Caruso flipped his phone shut and took a sip of his soda as he settled back into his chair, his bait-less fishing rod settled between his knees. This was beginning to feel like a huge mistake, but then they had little choice. Their partnership with the old man was tentative at best and the most he could hope for was that it would end soon. And since he wasn't in the habit of leaving loose ends he intended to do it right this time. When the time came, the partnership would be terminated along with the partner. For now, he would continue to think about greener pastures and projects that didn't include an elusive and overprotective boss.

Caruso heard the engine before he saw it.

He sat up straighter in his chair as a green and white fishing boat made its way around the point and into the small island inlet. He put a hand up to shield his eyes as he watched the boat circled just offshore from the island. Maybe, they were just pulling a line of traps and would soon be on their way.

He reached down, picking up the binoculars and leveling his gaze at the boat. No such luck, the man was pulling on a wet suit and gathering up diving apparatus. It looked like he intended to stick around for a while.

This wasn't good. The last thing they needed was a witness when it came time to pick up the drop.

He watched through the binoculars as the man on the boat slipped on a mask and hoisted a tank onto his back and levered himself on the edge of the boat before going over into the water. It looked like he had no intention of leaving anytime soon and that was too bad, because now they were going to have to do something about him.

Caruso nudged Taimon who was dozing in the seat next to him and handed him the binoculars, nodding in the direction of the newly arrived lobster boat. Taimon set the binoculars down and nodded at Caruso. Without a word they were already in agreement. They both knew what had to be done.

Caruso reeled in his line and pulled the anchor as Taimon fired up the boat's engine.

With one last glance toward the island, Caruso reached inside his jacket and pulled his gun out of the shoulder holster. There was never such a thing as an uncomplicated job.

Jamie picked his way up the gravel path worn next to the shore. The sun was making its descent beyond the trees. He hadn't found out much today, but maybe tonight he'd have better luck. He intended on talking with some of the locals to see what he could find out. Maybe one of them would give him some sort of a clue that would lead him in the right direction.

He stopped, admiring the view. Rocks sheltered a small beach that faced out onto the Atlantic. Pine trees edged the deep sides of the cliffs making it feel even more isolated. He breathed in the fresh salt air. If he were a pirate it would have been a perfect place to hide a treasure. Remote and reclusive, it was a private sanctuary. The perfect place to do whatever was needed without being seen.

Lobster buoys were clustered in the shallow water near to shore and spread out more as the water deepened. He looked out at the numerous islands filling the harbor. There was any number of places someone could hide. Some of them were covered with trees and brush; others were just rough outcroppings of rocks and seaweed. Maine islands had been hiding places for centuries. It wouldn't be too hard for someone to disappear into the scenery and not be found for quite some time.

He scanned the horizon and sighed. Somehow, he'd hoped to find more.

He turned and started to make his way back down the rocks when something in the seaweed caught his attention. It was a package with brown matte butcher paper, beneath a covering of shrink-wrapped plastic. He picked it up. It was small, maybe no more than ten inches long and wide and secured with thick plastic-coated flexible wire. A rope, like the heavy kind used for trap lines, had been secured to the wire with duct tape that trailed off into the water. He pulled on the end of the rope and was able to reel in about ten feet of it before the line came to an abrupt end. He eyed the end of the rope. It was cut clean with some sort of knife. There were no rough edges where it would have worn through with age and wear and no fraying of the twines. Jamie straightened up and looked around once again. The only other sign of life was a lobster boat circling offshore a ways.

Someone had taken a lot of trouble to make sure that whatever was inside stayed waterproof. And since tying it to the end of a rope line and sinking it wasn't something he usually saw then whatever was inside had to be important. Either way, he wasn't about to leave it behind for someone else to find and he wasn't about to stick around and take any chances that someone could be watching his discovery.

He watched as the lobster boat circled closer and he was able to see that there were two men aboard. The best thing would be to take it someplace secure to investigate further.

He reached into his pocket and pulled out his penknife. Crouching down next to the package he worked his knife through the rope leaving the rest to slide back into the ocean as he stuffed the box under his coat.

Chapter Six

Someone was still awake.

A light was on in the kitchen window as he walked toward the boarding house. He muttered a curse. He'd been hoping to slip in unnoticed.

He'd stuffed the package into his saddlebag. Right now, the only thing he wanted to do was to go into his rented room and find some privacy where he could take a good look at its contents.

He cut across the backyard, where the light from the back door didn't quite reach the far corners of the yard, and stood there for a moment waiting for a glimpse of someone at the windows, but saw no one. He moved closer to the house and stepped up to the back door, easing open the screen so that it wouldn't screech as he stepped into the mudroom.

There was no sound from inside and no one in the kitchen. With a little luck he wouldn't run into anyone on the way to his room.

He struggled to make his steps as quiet as possible on the old linoleum floor, limping a little. His injured leg throbbed in protest. He hadn't been this tired or ached this much since he'd been in the hospital.

He braced his weight against the doorjamb to the kitchen and off his sore leg. He had a strong premonition that whatever was in that package could be the key to the whole damned thing.

"Oh, it's you." Shelby stood in the darkened living room, a look of disappointment on her face.

"What is it? What's wrong?" Jamie let the saddlebag slide to the floor.

Shelby's eyes were large and translucent, her face ashen white, like a little lost girl. His heart flip-flopped in his chest. No matter how much he wanted to distance himself from any personal connection he may feel for her, he couldn't ignore the fear on her face.

"It's my brother, Josh. His boat isn't in yet and there hasn't been any word from him. We've checked everywhere we can think of, but there is no sign of him."

He could hear the unspoken fear and desperation in her voice and recognized the look of quiet hope in her eyes. He'd seen the same kind of fear more times than he cared to remember. It was a part of the job, but somehow this time it was all the more personal to him because it was coming from her.

He pulled out one of the matching vinyl-covered chairs, motioning for her to sit next to him. She slid into the chair, and he sat down next to her, their knees touching beneath the table.

"He's stayed out before without calling in, hasn't he? Maybe he put in somewhere else and just didn't call to let you know. He doesn't appear to be the most reliable person," he said.

Shelby twirled a piece of ragged napkin in her hand, worrying it until it was wasted.

"Maybe you're right. I'm sure you're right. My brother doesn't always think when he should." She shrugged. "I can't explain this worry. I just know that something isn't right. It feels just like it did when . . ." Her words trailed off, hanging in the air between them. She was trying to convince herself and not doing a very good job of it.

"Just like when?" Lord help him, there was something about this woman that drew him in. He reached down and captured her fidgeting fingers between his, stilling them with his own. "Tell me when it was like."

"It feels very much the same as when my husband disappeared." All the power in her body escaped from her like air deflating from a balloon. Her shoulders sagged in defeat and the edge of her lower lip quivered.

He'd done it now. He wasn't going to be able to back away when she needed help.

He thought of the package in his bag. He'd waited this long. A few more minutes wasn't going to make that much difference.

The old radio on the hall table crackled and hissed slicing through the tension in the room, but nothing decipherable could be heard.

"Where is your uncle? Does he know what is going on?"

Shelby shook her head. "He's out in the skiff looking for him. He left about an hour ago. But with sunset he doesn't have much luck of finding him. Josh's last call was around two-thirty. He dropped off the guy that lobsters with him and was going out to try some diving, but he only had enough air to be down for twenty minutes. I didn't speak with the guy. But he said that Josh told him he'd seen something odd off of Hen Island and he was going to take a look."

Jamie forced himself to keep from stiffening. If Josh wasn't involved with the illegal activity, but had managed to see something he shouldn't have, then his life was in danger. With Caruso and Taimon sitting off the coast it was a sure bet that they were up to something in the area. And if Josh had gotten involved with those two, then he was in just as much danger as if he had stumbled upon something by accident. Either way, Josh was in way over his head.

"Just how late is he? When should he have been in?"

Shelby turned to glance at the old clock on the stove. "About four hours ago."

Jamie got up from the table and crossed over to the old black phone hanging on the wall. He picked up the receiver, dialing the number he had committed to memory.

"What are you doing?"

Jamie ignored her question for the moment. He had so much speculation running through his head that he was almost afraid to speak, afraid that he would say too much. He was going to have to be careful about how he reacted to it all or he could attract some very unwanted attention.

"I have a friend at the Coast Guard station in Boothbay. I think he can help." He turned his back to her as he waited for the connection to go through. He couldn't look at her and still keep his thoughts together.

"Kearsage. It's me, Rivard. We need assistance on a search off Chandler. The owner left from Chandler this morning to haul trap lines and then dropped off his sternman to go do some diving around fourteen hundred hours. He could be around the Hen Island area."

"Man, what in the hell have you gotten yourself into this time, Rivard? First, you show out of the blue, and then you call me about a late boat?" There was a huge sigh on the other end of the line. "And I bet I'm not supposed to ask questions."

"Affirmative. The kid should have arrived back four hours ago. He has a history of being late, but his last call was around fourteen-thirty. He was going to do some urchin diving and his sister believes he only had enough air to go for a short dive. She also hasn't been able to raise him, either on the radio, or phone."

"I'll put it through. He must have a death wish diving by himself." There was a rustle of paper on the other end of the line. "Okay, go ahead, give me the info on him."

Jamie tried to think of what he knew about Josh, but his details were sketchy. He held the receiver away from him. "Shelby, I'm going to need some particulars to give them."

He relayed the information as she gave it to him, repeating it into the receiver, avoiding looking into her eyes because he knew he'd see questions there that couldn't be answered. Right now, there was a sort of numbed acceptance in her, but once she came out of her state of worry there were bound to be questions. Questions that he wasn't ready to answer.

Right now she was dealing with the stress and anxiety of her brother's disappearance, but she was smart. Once things settled down, he was going to have one hell of a time trying to explain his way out of this.

He listened as Kearsage came back on the line with an update. They were sending out a boat to do an initial search and they would go from there.

"Those favors are getting thin, Rivard. A few more of these and we are both going to be in trouble." His friend laughed, but they both knew Jamie was pushing it with every contact he made.

"Yes, I understand. Thanks for the help. Add what I owe you to my tab and let us know if you hear anything." He gave the telephone number and then hung up.

He took a deep breath and turned to face

her questioning look. He knew he had just added more to the mystery of the evening, but right now was not the right time to tell her the whole truth, even if he could risk it.

"They're going to send a search boat to the area and they'll be in touch as soon as they find anything." He hesitated to say "when they find Josh" because he wasn't at all sure that they would. He was having another one of his intuitive moments and it was scaring the hell out of him. That inkling of premonition was hitting him somewhere at the base of his neck and that almost always spelled trouble. He could usually count on it to mean something big.

"How did you . . . ?"

He'd expected that question.

"It's nothing. I have a friend in Boothbay that I went to school with, who's stationed at the Coast Guard station here. We've been in touch off and on and he doesn't mind helping me out."

She nodded, confusion showing in her eyes. But his answer would just have to be enough for now.

His problem was that he couldn't clear Shelby of all suspicion in his mind. So far, he'd found nothing to indicate she was involved, nor that she had any knowledge of any illegal activity. His heart was telling him that she wasn't involved. He just wasn't sure he could trust his heart.

He looked around at the old, comfortable house. There was no obvious sign of sudden wealth. Shelby's nature was open, even trusting to a fault. And except for their first meeting she had been friendly. There wasn't much to cast suspicion on Shelby.

But he couldn't say the same about her uncle, or her missing brother.

"You'll need to stay by the phone in case they need to contact you." If they find him, he added to himself. "In a couple of hours, you should know something more. I would suggest you get hold of your uncle and have him here with you." He picked up his gear from the edge of the table and held it in his hands. He needed something to do; otherwise, he might be tempted to try and comfort her.

Vulnerability was mirrored in her eyes. She was as clear as a thin piece of glass and one stiff wind would shatter her into a thousand pieces.

She got to her feet and came to stand close to him. So close he could smell the faint scent of her shampoo and see the faint smattering of freckles across her nose. He forced himself to keep his hands at his side. Shelby was a complication. At least, that was what he was going to keep telling himself until it sunk in.

"Thank you. I don't know what to say."

He shifted from foot to foot to ease the ache in his leg and uncomfortable feeling settling in his stomach. He wasn't comfortable taking thanks from people, even when it was part of his job. He'd never been very good at playing hero. It just wasn't in his nature. He was a renegade; at least he liked to think of himself that way.

Still, he wasn't as hard around the edges as he would like to imagine himself. It only took someone like Shelby, to show him that he was just as susceptible to a soft heart and human emotions as the next guy. Maybe more so in her case.

Geez, he needed to get out of there and get a drink.

"No thanks are needed. I just happened to be wearing my white hat tonight." He moved around her and started for the hallway leading to his room.

"Wait. Where are you going?"

He looked back. She was watching him. The little voice inside him kept telling him to turn around and go back.

"I need to go out for a while. I promised someone I would meet them." He could see the dejection in her face. Someone should stay with her to help her and wait with her.

But he couldn't be that person. He had to keep reminding himself that he was here for a reason. It was his job to find out who was behind the activity in Chandler and that meant he needed to keep his professional distance. No matter that what he really wanted to do was to turn around and take her in his arms and comfort her like a child with a nightmare, or a woman with a soft body.

"Oh, I understand." He was a heel for running out, but he needed to put some fast distance between himself, the situation, and her.

She wiped at a tear on her cheek and Jamie clenched his fists tighter around the gear in his hand. He fought the urge to go to her and brush the tears away for her. But then again, he'd been fighting a lot of urges since he had met her.

"I'm not very good at handling situations like this, Shelby. I'm sorry." He slung his bag over his shoulder. He needed to be out of here, for more reasons than one. In a very short while, all hell was going to break loose and he needed to be as far away from here as he could get. "I need to go." He started again down the hall toward his room. He didn't dare look back this time. He didn't want to see her watching him. If he did, he knew he'd end up going back and doing what he really wanted to do.

He stepped into his room, closing the door behind him and leaning against it for a minute.

He was going to have to put off his exploration of the package until things cooled down. Right now, he needed to get out of here in case someone from the Coast Guard showed up. He couldn't risk anyone recognizing him. He had already risked enough this evening by calling Kearsage.

If they did find Josh safe then Shelby would have her happy ending. But if they found him injured or, worse, if they didn't find him at all, then there would be questions.

Questions he wasn't prepared to answer.

He was here to do his job. He needed to check on the list of possible suspects that McAlvey had given him and find out if any of them had been involved with suspicious activity. Time was running out.

He stashed his gear and the package in the top corner of the clothes closet in his room and placed a folded quilt over it to hide it.

The ache in his leg reminded him of how far he still had to go. He threw himself onto the bed, propping his leg up on a pillow as he stared up at the ceiling. His body sank into the soft comfort of the old mattress as he fought to release some of the tension centered between his shoulders.

It was so easy for him to slip into his role of rescuer that he had almost given himself and his cover away. He'd been playing rescuer all of his life whether he wanted to, or not.

He needed to get himself back on track. Frustrated, he got up and pulled his dark-colored windbreaker over his head. Grabbing a flashlight from his pack, he slipped out into the hall.

There were no sounds in the house. Maybe Shelby had gone down to the wharf to look for her uncle or maybe she had gone out onto the deck to wait. He slipped out the back door and across the lawn. It was so quiet that he could hear his footsteps in the grass. Even the ocean was quiet tonight and the crickets had stopped their songs.

He straddled his bike, turned the key, switched on the gas and hit the start button. The engine roared to life and the stillness of the night gave way to the rattle of the bike's exhaust pipes.

He was doing the right thing. Walking away was the logical choice. He would let the Coast Guard handle finding her brother and let Shelby handle her own worries.

Right now, the best place to find information was at the local tavern.

There was enough light from the kitchen window to see Jamie as he made his way across the backyard. She hid in the shadow of the curtains, watching as he got on his motorcycle and prepared to leave.

Jamie Rivard was a contradiction. In the short time she had known him he had shown so many sides to him she wasn't quite sure which was his true nature.

What she did know was that she was grateful for his help tonight. Old fears had stopped her from taking the action that was needed and Jamie had taken over. Wherever Josh was, he had a better chance of getting back okay if immediate action was taken.

Anything could have happened to him. He could be stranded with a broken motor, or he could have put in somewhere else for the night. Any alternative was better than the thoughts that threatened to consume her. She refused to think that something more serious had happened to her brother. He was irresponsible and irrational at times, but he would never risk his life.

At least she hoped he wouldn't.

The sound of the motorcycle engine startled her from her thoughts. She looked out the window to find Jamie adjusting the controls of his bike as he shifted the bike under his weight.

His legs looked much too long to ride a motorcycle and for a moment an image flashed through her mind, of what it would be like to have him use his long muscled legs to keep her captive. She felt a rush of heat flush her cheeks. She was becoming strange. She shook her head and groaned. She was not going to have those kinds of thoughts about any man right now. She couldn't remember the last time she had even considered having thoughts about a man.

She looked out the window again as he steered his bike out of the driveway and up the road. The sound of his tires crunching on the gravel faded into the distance.

It had been so long since Tommy's death. Maybe her body and mind were reminding her that she was still alive. But Jamie Rivard was not the man to give her a wake-up call. He was an attractive man and, despite his obvious reluctance, he had a good nature about him. Still, the sooner he left Chandler, the better it would be for everyone.

She pulled her coat from the hook behind

the door and grabbed her cordless phone, before letting herself out onto the deck. The night air was crisp and clear and the fresh breeze wrinkling the trees foreshadowed the true fall weather.

She settled into one of the Adirondak chairs facing out over the shore and watched the lights shining from the houses along the water. Inside those houses, all of the people were safe and secure with their families. They were busy putting kids to bed and having quiet time with the people they loved. And she was alone.

She pushed back again at the tears that were near the surface. Once this was all settled and her brother was home safe and sound she was going to find herself a life.

The heavy sound of footsteps echoed through the house. The screen door banged behind her and she looked up to find her uncle. In the darkness, she searched his gaze for any hopeful sign that Josh was safe. But all she could see was the tight, tired line of his lips and the grim look in his eyes. It was bad. Her stomach settled around her feet and she fought the surge of panic that threatened to overwhelm her. She could read the look on his face. It was the same one he had given her when Tommy had disappeared.

"What is it?" Her words echoed hollow in her ears.

"It's Josh." He came to place a comforting hand upon her shoulder and she knew, without a doubt, that he wasn't coming with good news this time.

"They found his boat anchored off of Hen Island. He is missing and so is most of his dive gear. I'm afraid that it doesn't look good."

With a cry, she launched herself out of the chair and into the comfort of his arms, enveloping herself in his strength as she let out the tears and the fear.

Callaway's Pub wasn't much of a pub. It was small, dark and almost vacant at the ungodly hour of ten o'clock on a Tuesday night. It was just the kind of place that he would have picked if he had been here for any other reason.

High stools were lined up against a wooden bar and music was playing from an unseen jukebox near the back of the narrow room. Behind the bar, the low hum of a two-way radio fought for attention with the noise of a television hanging on the wall.

Jamie settled down onto one of the stools and motioned to the bartender to bring him a beer. Two old fishermen at the bar, their heads bent toward each other, were in deep, quiet conversation. Nothing wrong here that he could see.

The two old men at the counter turned and eyed him, sizing him up. He nodded in greeting and they nodded back before resuming their talk. He could hear snatches of their conversation; bits and pieces punctuated by their thick Maine accents. They were deep in discussion over cut lines and lost traps. Someone had been encroaching on someone else's territory and it wasn't settling well in the small town.

The bartender set a beer in front of him. He was a tall, thin man who looked to be in his late fifties. His dark hair was spiky and straight and he had a graying handlebar mustache under a hawk-like nose. His hesitant gaze inspected him from behind a pair of wire-rimmed glasses.

"You're new around here. Where are you from?"

Jamie took a sip of beer before answering. "Born and raised in New Orleans. But more recently I'm from the Key West area." He reached for a handful of the nuts in the chipped bowl on the bar and tossed a couple into his mouth.

"Sounds like you get around."

"I guess I do. I thought I'd check out

Maine for a change." This was a test of sorts. He knew that if he were going to get any information then he would have to either fit in or, at best, be judged as a non-threat.

"Well, if you are looking for night life, mister, Chandler ain't got any. You've come at the busy time and you can see what it's like right now. Most times, people who want excitement head into Portland. Around here the only excitement is when someone gets a hangnail." He started wiping down the bar with a wet rag.

"I'm not here for excitement. I'm here to work." The bartender stilled his wiping. Jamie's words had somehow hit a hitch.

"It's mighty hard to find a job around here. It's mostly families working with families and such. You might do better finding a job down to Rockland, or Camden. I hear they like to hire your kind, a lot." Jamie ignored the offhanded comment and continued munching on the nuts.

"I already found a job. But I appreciate the advice." Again, the bartender stopped his wiping and looked at him over the rim of his glasses.

"Well, that's fairly fast. If'n you don't mind my asking, who gave you a job?"

"Case gave me a job hauling with him."

The bartender's eyes narrowed, as he looked Jamie up and down again, sizing him up. At the end of the bar, the two old men had stopped their conversation and were now listening to the exchange. He willed himself to keep from stiffening up. He hadn't wanted to call more attention to himself, but it would appear that he had. He had either just blown it royally or . . .

"I guess if Case gave you a job, then you must be all right. He's a good judge of character for someone from away."

He let out the breath he'd been holding. He'd passed inspection, at least for the time being. Now, all he had to do was ask some questions without raising their suspicions all over again.

The door opened with a gust of wind that rocked the curtains at the window. A young man in his twenties came into the bar and sidled up next to him. His worn shirt, faded jeans and rubber boots marked him as a local.

"Hey Callaway, what's with all of the action down at the wharf?" The conversation in the bar stopped, as all eyes turned to the newcomer. Jamie stayed rooted to his seat and took a drink of his beer, trying his damnedest to fade into the woodwork.

"Something is going on down at the wharf?"

The young man's head bobbed up and down. He was dying to tell what he knew.

"There's a bunch of trucks and people down at the wharf and I heard on the radio that they called out Search and Rescue from Portland. It must be bad."

"Any idea who it is?" The bartender shuffled over behind the bar and fiddled with the knobs on the radio. "Geez, I didn't have a clue there was anything going on. I've had the radio turned down all day. The constant cackling was driving me crazy." The crackling static of the radio rose with the increased volume.

The radio conversations were stilted at first, the voices hard for Jamie to decipher. But it was clear that the others in the bar were familiar with voices. The tones were hurried and the words precise. Everyone in the bar was now crowded around the radio, drawn by the tension filtering through the airwaves.

"I can't believe it. I can't believe that young fool is missing."

"Roe, who's missing?" The young man next to him touched one of the old men on the arm as he spoke. He could hear the concern in his voice and inside he could feel his own chest tightening. With every word transmitted, the tension was mounting in the bar. All unnecessary conversation stopped as everyone leaned closer to hear the radio.

The words were garbled as they came across. He caught bits of conversation here and there, enough to know that what they had found wasn't good news. The *Glory Days* had been located anchored off a local island with no sign of Josh. Just what he had feared.

Jamie looked out the window. The wind had begun to pick up, scattering the leaves on the trees. With a little luck the clouds would clear up with the wind. They could use the light from a bright moon to search for a while more before giving up for the night.

The best scenario would be if Josh had somehow made it to one of the nearby islands for safety. Even with the recent mild temperatures, the water was much too cold to spend any length of time in it. If he had on a survival suit or a wet suit then his chances were better, but from the sound of it, they hadn't found him or his diving gear. This didn't sound very good.

He moved over a couple of the stools to be closer to the others. The two older men were now talking low among themselves, shaking their heads as they listened to the information coming through.

"I told you that we shoulda' seen this coming."

Jamie leaned closer across the bar toward them.

"I told you that there was something funny going on. And now that young idiot has gone and turned up missing. Shelby had enough to worry about already. Now, Josh has added his lot to it." One of the old men shook his head and pushed the worn cap further back on his head. Weathered lines of age covered the hard planes of the old fisherman's face. Years of hauling traps had left him with a permanent bronzed tan and his hands were gnarled and pointy.

"You mean the diving?" He tried to keep a schooled casual look to his face. The two old men turned to look at him.

"No, though that's cussid enough reason. I mean that things haven't been right around these parts for a while now and when everything gets out of kilter, then someone is gonna get hurt."

"Well, what was it that made it so weird?" He knew that he was pushing. But they knew more than what they were saying.

"I mean, that all of a sudden, people who

don't have no money are starting to get some fancy ideas. Boats that were running right before, ain't running at all now and there has been some strange kind of stuff that people been seeing and it ain't no UF an O's. Maybe we just got too many outsiders for a town as small as Chandler." The old man bit down on the cigar that hung unlit from his jaw.

Jamie downed the last of his beer and pushed it and a tip back across the bar. He nodded again at the bartender as he headed for the door. But his departure went unnoticed as everyone crowded around the bar to hear the latest news on the radio.

He stepped out the door into the night. The only light came from the single bulb on the bar's painted sign and the glow coming through the faded curtains and dirty windows of the bar.

Pulling the collar of wind jacket up a little higher for protection, he hunched his shoulders to stay warm. The night air was cold and crisp and had a snap to it as he took in a deep ragged breath.

Their welcome to him had been better than he had expected. He hadn't expected to be accepted so easily and his guess was that it had to do with his association with Case. The man was an outsider and yet somehow he had managed to gain respect from the locals. Not an easy thing to do. His grudging acceptance had given him the opportunity to see their reactions to Josh's disappearance. They had run the gamut from casual disinterest to outright speculation over the event. But that was to be expected in such a situation. He had done enough speculating himself.

The one piece he had found most interesting was the old man's reluctance to expand on his suspicions. Either he was being tight-lipped or most of them had already speculated on where the money was coming from.

While Josh's disappearance made him less of a suspect, Jamie wasn't ready to take him off the list, just yet. He had heard the argument between Shelby and her brother, and that was enough for him to be suspicious about where Josh's money was coming from.

He stepped off the porch and heard the crunch of gravel under his feet. His bike was parked at the edge of the parking lot, closest to the road. He'd look into a few more things and then he was going to throw himself into that bed and get some much-needed rest.

That's when he heard other footsteps in the dirt. The hair at the back of his neck stood up. It was that premonition thing, again.

Nobody else had come or gone out of the bar since he had left and he hadn't seen anyone around when he had walked out.

He forced himself to keep walking and not tense up. He didn't want to alert whoever it was that he was aware they were behind him. He considered his options. With the noise from the radio in the bar, he doubted that anyone would hear him and come to his rescue.

The road was deserted. There was little chance of anyone happening along to help him at this hour. There wasn't a light on anywhere. Most of the town was in bed for the night.

He lengthened his stride as much as he could without making it obvious. The sound of footsteps behind him increased and got louder. He was halfway across the parking lot, calculating the distance between him and the bike and whoever was just behind his right shoulder.

Damn, not enough time.

He had no other choice. Friend or foe he was going to have to turn and find out just who was behind him.

He counted to himself. One. Two. Three.

Turn.

The first thing he noticed was a wall of flesh that towered over his own six-foot-three frame. The next thing that he noticed was that there was not one, but two of these mountains of flesh. One was smaller than the first, but no less imposing in size.

Double damn.

"This him?" he heard the deep rusty voice that sank his stomach to his feet as one giant nodded to another.

Time slowed to a merciless crawl as Jamie watched the mammoth figure before him pull back his arm in a wide arc, gaining momentum. In that instant, Jamie heard a sharp yell in the distance, but his mind processed only two clear thoughts: this was going to hurt like hell — and someone had sent these goons out looking for him.

Chapter Seven

"What the . . . ?"

Jamie's head was buzzing and his jaw felt like it was padded with cotton. His fuzzy brain began clearing up fast as the sound of heavy footsteps and shouting grew closer.

He willed himself to lie still while he struggled to regain his bearings. Bits of gravel dug into his back as the sharp edge of a rock pierced his shoulder blades. Already a lump was forming on the back of his thickheaded skull.

This was where he had landed. Damned if he hadn't gone out cold. It had been years since someone had managed to get so much over on him so fast. But then it had been a long time since someone the size of a truck had hit him. He kept his eyes shut and willed his body to stay relaxed as he adjusted to the noises around him.

He wanted to make damn sure that the coast was clear before anyone noticed that he was already conscious. He wasn't ready to face a guy that size again, yet.

The shouting and footsteps stopped.

There was a rustle of clothing as someone bent over him. He forced his breathing to remain calm.

"You all right?" Jamie opened his eyes at the sound of Case's voice.

"I think so, if you don't count the truck that just hit me." With much effort he managed to raise himself into a sitting position, rubbing at the bump that was rising on the back of his head.

"From the look of the two I just saw leaving, I would say that you make some mighty big and mean friends." Case helped him struggle to his feet.

"If those tree trunks were my friends, then I'd hate to see my enemies. You didn't happen to get a good look at them did you?" Jamie wavered for a moment before he regained his balance. This was going to hurt in the morning. Hell, it hurt right now. He put his fingers to his jaw and felt the soreness and puffiness.

"You mean you don't know them?"

Jamie just shook his head. "I haven't been here long enough to make enemies like those two. My guess is that they must have just hated the sight of me."

He wasn't about to tell Case that there was any number of people who could resent his being in Chandler. One of them might even be him.

"I'm just glad you came along when you did," Jamie said. "Who knows what kind of condition I'd be in if you hadn't sent them running."

"You just need to learn to pick on guys your own size, Rivard." He crossed his arms over his massive chest.

"I'll have to remember that for next time." Jamie rubbed at the sore spot a bit longer.

"It wasn't just by accident that I came looking for you, Rivard. I need to ask a favor of you."

Well, this could be interesting. "Sure, shoot . . ." He struggled to find his balance as he got to his feet. "Anything I can do to help . . ." And hopefully, something that would give him a lead.

"I need you to head back to the boarding house and keep an eye on Shelby for me."

"Is something wrong?"

Case stuffed his hands in his pockets and squared his shoulders, giving him a scrutinizing. Jamie leveled his gaze back at him, unflinching. "I just came in from the wharf. They found Josh's boat, but they still haven't found him."

"No sign at all?"

Case shook his head. "None. The damned fool has disappeared off the face of the earth. The Coast Guard is already on scene. As near as they can tell the boat is untouched. Except, most of the diving gear is missing."

"What do you mean by 'most' of the gear missing?"

Case looked out at the darkness beyond the ring of light illuminating them. "The only diving gear that they found on board was his best tank, the one he usually uses, and that one had twenty minutes of air left in it. The other tank had a faulty valve on it." His words were gruff and Jamie could feel the tension behind his words.

"Well, if they found the tank then he must not have been diving."

Case shook his head. "But the rest of gear, his flippers, his wetsuit, his mask, they were all missing off the boat."

"Well, maybe there is another explanation. Maybe he was snorkeling off one of the islands and got stranded." There were any number of islands where he could be holed up, waiting out the storm.

"Well, that's what the Coast Guard is hoping for. Unfortunately, with the high seas and the storm coming in, if they don't find something soon they're going to have cancel the search for a while."

Neither of them needed to add the rest of that ominous news. The longer Josh went unfound, the less likely of recovering him in one piece.

"So, you'll check on her for me? I'd like to help out with the search, but given what happened to her husband I think the wharf is the last place Shelby should be."

Jamie thought about all the reasons he had not to go back to that house tonight. There were a million reasons that he shouldn't be there, and yet, those reasons didn't mean a damn when he knew that she needed him.

"I'll do it. I just have to make a stop by the store first."

Taimon was worthless, Caruso decided. He had size and the intimidation factor, but he was short on brains. Taimon held his revolver in hand as they stood in the shadow of the old vacant cannery. The black metal caught and glinted in the minimal moonlight they had to work with.

"Put that thing away, you idiot," Caruso said. "You've caused enough problems for me tonight. I told you to take care of Rivard and you didn't finish the job. Now we need to lay low here for a while in case that other guy got a good look at us. I only hope he can't finger us."

"Rivard didn't see a thing. He couldn't have. He was too busy kissing the ground. I would have finished him off, if the other guy hadn't charged at us, yelling and swinging. He made enough noise to wake the dead." Taimon stuffed the gun back into his waist harness and folded his arms across his chest in an impatient gesture.

"If you'd done your job, it wouldn't have mattered if Rivard had seen you or not. Now, we not only have to worry about whether or not Rivard got a good look at us, but whether the other guy can ID us." Caruso was going to have to do some fast thinking, if he was going to turn this around.

"I don't see what you're worried about. We'll just finish him off the next time. For now, we just stay here until we can slip back to the boat." Taimon pulled a knife from his belt and began running the sharp tip beneath his fingernails.

Caruso stepped forward until his face was just a few scant inches from Taimon's. Taimon tended to be a bit of a loose cannon when left on his own. So, it was up to him to make it clear who was in charge and what their objective was.

"You idiot, we are sitting on a huge

amount of trouble that has yet begun to pay off. If we are going to pull this off, then we can't take a chance of getting the old man mad. Right now, he controls the flow of inventory in and out. Without him we are out of business."

Taimon met him eye to eye, but he could see a faint flicker in his look. Taimon knew that what he was saying was true. Without the old man they were out of business and sitting on a potential time bomb.

"We just have to be patient and find a way to get rid of Riv-ard without making everyone else suspicious," Caruso said, thinking aloud. "After the flub up at the bar someone is bound to be on the lookout for us."

"We'll get him," Taimon said, not really concerned. "After all, how hard can it be in a dive as small as Chandler?"

Caruso just shook his head. Taimon didn't understand. He was used to the city, used to anonymity that places like Miami offered.

He started running through his options in his head. Before they could go after Rivard again, they had something else they needed to do.

"There is no chance of us doing the pickup tonight. Fouling up this job has just screwed up our chances of collecting the drop. Besides, we still haven't gotten word on what to do with them when we get them. I heard on the radio that the Coast Guard is in the area looking for a lost fisherman. We'll just have to lay low for a day or two until they're done." He let out a tired sigh. "Next time we'll just have to make sure we finish Rivard off for good."

It was past midnight by the time Jamie made his way up the back steps of the boarding house. He stopped at the door, listening for sounds from within. There were none.

His roundabout trip back had taken him to the store where he had used Shelby's radio to monitor the Coast Guard frequency. High winds and rough seas were hampering the search and when a distress call came in off Georgetown, the search for Josh had been called for the night.

It was a tough call. One that he knew from experience was heartbreaking to make. There was nothing worse than knowing that there could be someone out there who needed your help and there wasn't a damn thing you could do about it.

They would resume the search in the morning. Still, the chances of finding him were fading more and more with each hour. The National Weather Service had long since changed their forecast from a hurricane watch to a warning, telling those along the New England coast to prepare for the storm that was bearing down on them. With the increased tides, wind, rain and waves there would be no way they could continue the search.

And that was the precise reason he had gone into Special Ops instead of search and rescue. He had done some time pulling people from the water, but his own past had made the failures too hard to deal with. It was easy to get burned out emotionally dealing with the consequences of situations like these. He hated the responsibility of having to explain why they couldn't save someone. The worst part of the job was telling the family when an operation had failed.

After a while, the pressure had taken a toll on him. He could deal with the trafficking. There wasn't a better feeling than when they busted someone for drugs or running guns. It was a natural high, just knowing that he was helping take drugs off the streets. But it was the other side he hated. It was the hopelessness of what he couldn't control. He had joined the Coast Guard to help people, not give up on them.

He went after the bad guys face to face.

He dealt with the known, instead of the unknown, and he found satisfaction in taking them off the market. It was a small reward to know that he may have helped someone.

He carefully swung open the screen door and let himself into the mudroom. The only light came from the clock on the oven, but it was enough to guide him.

Shelby must have decided to turn in; which could only mean that she had heard that the search had been abandoned for the night. The house was quiet as he headed down the hallway to his room. And then, he heard the noise. It was soft and low, an indefinable murmur cascading across him. The familiar prick of the skin at the back of his neck alerted his senses. He ran a hand under the edge of his jacket to his gun holster, running his fingers across the grip.

He moved through the shadows of the living room, staying close to the wall as he searched the darkness for the origin of the noise.

And then, he heard it again. He turned toward the window and the direction of the sound and his gaze fell on a figure huddled against the cushions of the window seat.

Strained moonlight, muted by the lacey fall of curtains at the window, fell over her hunched, huddled figure. Shelby's hair had swung forward covering her face. Her knees were pulled up tight in front of her as she rested her head on her arms. Jamie eased his hand from the grip of his gun and let out a sigh of relief, willing his body to relax as he leaned against the wall and tried to slow his breathing.

He'd been worried about her. The afterthought struck him just as hard as his earlier hit. Creeping through the darkened house looking for burglars was one thing, but he'd be a fool if he didn't acknowledge that his mind had been on Shelby's safety.

If he were a smart man he would go back to his room and forget that he had seen her. Heck, if he were a smart man he wouldn't have agreed to come back and keep watch over her.

He should leave. He'd promised Case to look out for her, but comforting Shelby could be more of a complication. She was a self-reliant and determined woman and he respected her for it. But there was an edge of vulnerability underneath her resilient exterior that struck something within him. Shelby could take care of herself. So why was it that he found himself feeling responsible for making sure she was all right?

Shelby Teague was a complication he

didn't need right now. He was here to solve a problem and damned if he wasn't going to do just that. He owed it to himself and to David to get through this and find out what had happened to him. He couldn't give up now. Finding out what was going on in Chandler was his ticket to finding out the truth about what really had happened to David.

He didn't have any other choice.

He turned to make his way back down the hall to his room when he heard her hiccup. That one small vulnerable sound convinced his heart to change his mind. There was no way he could walk away and leave her crying. He just didn't have it in him.

He walked over to stand beside her at the window. Sensing his presence, she raised her head and the meager light coming through the windows traced the wet track of tears streaking her cheeks. She brushed at the tears with the back of her hand as she sat up straighter on the window seat and tucked her feet up under her.

"Oh sorry, I didn't know you were there. I was just . . ." Her words trailed off as she tried to stifle yet another hiccup, and failed.

"It's okay." He felt like an idiot. He didn't know the right words to say to her. He had spent his life trying to avoid situations like this. He just didn't have it in him.

"There's no word on Josh yet." Her words were small and quiet.

"I know. Your uncle tracked me down at Callaway's and told me." He left out the part about Case finding him lying prone on the ground and the fact that his face felt like it had been run over by a truck.

"You were at Callaway's?" And instantly, he felt like a heel. No doubt she thought that he was out drinking while she was struggling with her brother's disappearance. "Oh, well, good then. You're finding everything okay."

She looked up at him and he was glad for the anonymity of the darkness. He watched the gentle lift of her chin as she searched his face. Her lips were parted; her breath was coming out in small labored wisps as she fought against the emotions warring within her. And yet there was an almost defiant tilt to her shoulders. She would be okay.

He liked her lips. They were simple, classic, untouched by anything but the wind and time. He found himself imagining their softness, how they would feel against the tip of his finger. Unwanted sensation coursed through him at the mere thought of tracing the curve of her lips and lingering on the strong arch of their parting. He clenched his fists to his side.

Tonight only reinforced what he knew to be true. He wasn't here for a one-night stand, and Shelby and the other people of Chandler needed him to keep his head about him. He was here to do a job and if he was going to find out who was behind it all then he needed to keep his head straight. But more than anything, he needed to remember that he wasn't here to get side-lined by some determined, hard-nosed, beautiful woman with a soft mouth.

"Was the Coast Guard able to come up with anything?" He knew the answer, but he knew that he had to ask if only to keep up appearances.

"Nothing. They found his boat circling, but he wasn't on board." She turned to look out again at the water. Her voice was steady. Her words were calm.

He was right when he had called Shelby a survivor. She had been here before and survived. She would survive this as well, long after he was gone.

"They'll find something." It was the best he could offer without giving her false hope.

Shelby got up to pace the length of the living room. Her bare feet made no sound on the worn carpet. "The hardest part is just knowing that Josh is in danger and there isn't a damn thing I can do about it."

He had seen this all, a hundred times before. The endless searching for answers and the hopelessness of being stuck on the shore while the search went on at sea. He hated the feeling of helplessness and the inevitable waiting that came with each search.

"I'm sure they are doing everything they can." His words trailed off as he realized how futile they sounded. He'd said them so many times, and yet they were lame even to his own ears.

She stopped her pacing and looked up at him, her expression unreadable. "Yes, I am sure they are." She tried to manage a smile, but it faded as fast as it had appeared.

"It isn't as if I haven't been here before. I know the drill. I've paced this floor before. But I can't help wondering if . . ." Her words fell off, floating around them in the quiet. He knew the words that she couldn't bring herself to say. They were the words that could damn her brother's life and keep him from coming home again.

He wanted to say something to reassure her, but he had seen enough to know that he couldn't give her false hopes. She had already lost her parents and her husband.

Now, she could lose her brother.

She paced toward the window again, looking out over the water. The windows were open and he could hear the rhythmic lapping of the water washing ashore and the rustle of leaves in the swirling uplift of the breeze. The moonlight streaks of silver playing off against the small rippling waves.

A cell phone rang and he watched her pull the lighted phone from her pocket and flip it open.

"Hello?" There was silence as she listened to the caller. "Yes, I understand. First light. Okay." She hung up the phone.

The official call.

"That was the Coast Guard. They've called off the search due to the weather and they hope to start searching again at first light provided that the hurricane has blown by us by then." The words caught like a small cry in her throat.

"They said that they have searched all of the islands in the immediate area and come up with nothing. They are planning on sending divers down in the area in the morning provided the sea isn't too rough. With Hurricane Fenton threatening us they aren't sure just how much time we still have. They told me to stay put near the phone for now in case he should happen to call." Her words were factual, practiced as if she had rehearsed them in her head.

"We should know more sometime tomorrow." She let out a frustrated strangled sigh. "I wanted to go out on the boat with my uncle, but they all said I should stay here until word comes."

No matter what the word is, he added in his head. The chances of finding Josh alive and in good condition would diminish as the hours went by. Even with the unseasonably warm weather, the sea was still cold. His best chance would be if he could get to one of the small islands and find a place out of the elements. It was a small chance, but right now it was the only one they had.

Jamie needed to get more information about the search without blowing his own cover. He had already risked too much by calling the Coast Guard in. He needed to maintain his low profile. If someone were leaking information about seizure operations, then his cover would be at risk. There had to be another way to find out more, without being obvious.

"What are you going to do about the store?"

She let out a sigh. "I was going to shut it down for the day tomorrow, but I hate to do that. So many people around here depend on the store and me and with a storm heading our way they'll be in need of supplies." Her shoulders sagged under the weight of all she was handling.

"Why don't I help you run it? I don't know anything about running a store, but I'm sure I could help somehow." That way he could keep an ear to the gossip and maybe find out something that would help them all.

"You would do that for me?"

He closed the small distance between them standing next to her in the window. He didn't touch her, though he wanted to do just that. To touch her now would be to add a personal stake to all that was happening. He just couldn't risk Shelby or himself.

"Sure, how hard could working in the store be?"

A weak smile crossed her face. A fist of emotion turned in his stomach.

All of his resolve wavered as she put up a hand to his cheek, resting it there for a moment in a simple gesture of gratitude. The warmth of her fingers sent bolts of electricity coursing across his skin and, for a moment, he gave in to instinct and turned toward her touch, leaning against her fingers. He could give himself this one small gesture. It would have to last.

But Shelby surprised him as she stepped up on her toes and placed a soft kiss upon his cheek. Her warm lips grazed his bruised jaw and the trace of pain brought sent him slamming back to reality.

More than anything, he shouldn't be doing this. And, he definitely shouldn't be doing it with her. Letting her get close enough to touch him was a mistake. And yet, at this moment, it was what they both needed.

"I just want to thank you, Jamie. You have a way of being in just the right place, when you're needed." His hand covered hers as he brought it back down to her side. His fingers lingered for a moment against hers, before he pulled them back and stuffed them in his pockets.

He looked down into her eyes and was struck by the realization that all of his reserves were melting. Shelby Teague was open and trusting and she was putting her hopes into his hands.

She shook her head. "I don't know if I like you or not. You came charging into Chandler on that bike and I was sure that I disliked you. But now —" Her words trailed off for a second. "Now, I'm just not sure how I feel about you."

He used the moment to back up a step, putting badly needed distance between them as he laughed. "I have that effect on some people."

He had known Shelby Teague such a short time and she knew nothing about the real reason he was in Chandler. Besides, Shelby wasn't a casual relationship kind of woman. She was the kind you took home to mother. And the worst part was that this whole situation would have tickled his mother. Her runaway son, the reluctant one who always balked at any sign of a serious relationship, was thinking of stepping away from a beautiful woman out of respect for her. His mother, with her elegant manners and refined disposition, would have a field day trying to figure this one out.

"I'm sorry." He could see the confusion in her eyes. "I'm sorry if I made you uncomfortable by what I did. I wasn't trying to make you uncomfortable. I just wanted you to know how much I appreciate your help tonight." She clasped her hands in front of her and lowered her gaze. He felt like a heel.

"It's okay. Really." He forced a smile onto his face and willed his breathing to slow. Being attracted to Shelby was one thing, letting her know that he was attracted to her was a whole other affair. He needed to put some distance between them, fast.

"I guess that I'd better hit the hay. I'd suggest that you do the same."

She shook her head. "I think I'll sit up for a while. I don't think I can sleep."

She turned her back on him and walked back toward the window seat. He stood there for a moment, watching her. Damn, he wanted to touch her. He wanted to know what it felt like to hold her in his arms. He wanted to forget everything else and kiss her. But he couldn't.

He wasn't meant to care for this woman. It was the wrong time and the wrong place. He had a case to solve and when it was done, he'd be leaving Chandler, for good.

He watched her settle back into her corner of the window seat and pull a crocheted throw around her legs.

Hell, he knew what she was going through. The waiting and hoping was enough to shatter the strongest person. He'd been through the hell himself and it had made him the man that he was. It was also the reason he knew he would have to leave once this was all over. He wasn't made to be the kind of man that Shelby needed. She needed someone who could be there every day for her, supporting her, comforting her, and taking care of her. He wasn't that man.

Once the Coast Guard had called off the

search for the night, Caruso and Taimon were free to leave the old cannery and head back to where they had stashed the boat on the point.

In front of him, Taimon muttered a curse as his foot slipped on a clump of seaweed that was invisible in the darkness. They had stashed the boat in a vacant boathouse near the cove. Most of the summer people had left, which made the point a great place to go about their business unnoticed.

The wind was intensifying now, scattering the leaves from the trees and beating against them. Caruso pulled his jacket tighter around him, as he followed Taimon's big, dark form. Once at the boat, they would be able to make it out to the island and be able to warm up. But for now, they still needed to stay low and out of sight.

The old man wasn't going to be happy with them. They had botched things up today, royally. First, the young guy on the fishing boat, and then they'd screwed up with that Rivard guy.

Their orders were to take care of Rivard and they hadn't. Between the screw up and the weather, he could only speculate on what that would mean for their operation, now.

They were supposed to have a drop going

down tonight. He looked up at the fast moving clouds silhouetted against the blue-black sky. The forecast was bad. A hurricane was moving fast up the Atlantic and headed straight for them. They'd be lucky if the drop could take place at all. They were so close to the end of the operation that he was beginning to get nervous. Mistakes were being made. People were being careless. It would only take one small sighting to put them all out of business and behind bars for a very long time.

Caruso squinted into the darkness looking for the landmarks he had put to memory. They had reached the gray shingled house high up on the ledges, which meant that they were close to the boathouse. Warm light spilled from the wall of windows lining the waterside of the house. Whoever lived there was keeping late hours.

Caruso grabbed at the back of Taimon's jacket, pulling him down with him as a figure walked by the windows. They crouched there, hidden against the rocks as they waited for what felt like hours. The wind, water and darkness should be enough to hide them, but he wasn't taking any more chances tonight. He watched as the figure stopped at the window and raised a pair of binoculars.

Damn, what could they be looking for at this hour? What could they be looking for in the darkness? Unless?

He cursed again. He didn't need the complication of another nosy person adding to their already tough situation. If they were using binoculars at night, that meant that they were looking for someone or something. And that could only mean trouble.

Jamie had done what was asked of him. As promised, he'd made sure that Shelby was as okay as she could be under the circumstances.

It was easy for him to understand all of the emotions running through her. He understood the helplessness and the desperation.

But more than his experiences with his job, he knew what the pain was like on a personal level. He'd spent the weeks after David's death trying to figure out how to deal with his own feelings of helplessness and loss. McAlvey had been right about one thing. He'd been out of control, unable or unwilling to deal with David's death, but losing David had been the last in a very long line of losses. And he hadn't handled any of them very well.

Jamie vaulted off the bed and went to the

closet, rummaging through his bag. The house was quiet enough now and he'd put it off long enough. He needed to know just what was in the package he'd found at the point.

Pulling his jackknife from his belt, he cut through the gauged plastic and covered wire to the heavy paper. He used the edge of the knife to slit the tape holding it in place and peeled back the paper and plastic.

Damn. Now he knew why he was in Chandler. Or at least part of it.

He pulled a bandanna out of his pack and reached into the package, prying the foam packing material away, to pick up one of the matte, black objects. Draping the bandanna over his hand, he held it up. The sleek design glinted in the light from the single lightbulb dangling overhead.

Guns. He should have guessed. It was a logical choice. After all, they were small, neat and easy to conceal and profitable to smuggle. They were also fairly easy to obtain. He looked into the compact package. There were four more of the guns tucked inside. It was a small amount, enough not to garner too much attention if anyone bothered to look. He tested the weight and held it up to the light again. Whoever had packed the guns had taken the precaution of making sure there was nothing incriminating on them. He turned it over, searching for the serial numbers. There weren't any, not that he was surprised. Gun traffickers weren't about to leave anything behind that might lead investigators straight to them. And if the market for the guns was overseas then they weren't going to risk bringing international attention to what they were doing.

He set the gun back in the box and picked up a small, white folded sheet of paper at the bottom of the package. There were six words scribbled on the paper.

Filleann an feall ar an bhfeallaire.

He didn't know what it meant, but, with his limited knowledge of languages, it looked like it might be Irish.

He pulled his cell phone out of his pack. Right now, he needed to know what the note said and if anyone would know the translation, it would be Kearsage. And he would be able to get him the information without blowing his cover.

It was early morning now, but he knew that his friend would have the answer he needed. He punched in the number and waited for the connection.

Within minutes he had an answer. Eager to stretch his linguistic skills, Kearsage had been excited to offer his translation of the Irish proverb.

The treachery returns to the betrayer.

Outside the wind picked up with a gust, rattling the panes of the old window. He looked out at the night sky that was almost black. The frontal clouds from the hurricane were moving in on them fast. The tension from the coming storm crackled in him.

The real question was, who was the betrayer and what was the treachery?

Of course, it didn't take much to make the leap from an obscure Irish phrase to John Case. After all, he knew next to nothing about the man. Case had access to the wharf and to the harbor. Out on his boat, he could be running guns without calling any extra attention to himself. He had the opportunity. If he had a motive, it was most likely money. But there was one piece of the puzzle that didn't fit. If it were Case that was smuggling guns, would he really put Shelby and her brother into danger by doing it near them?

Chapter Eight

The weather forecast was bad, worse than they had first expected. Hurricane Fenton had picked up speed and was headed straight at them. At six in the morning, the storm surge was predicted to be enough to keep even the biggest boats in for the day and the Coast Guard had suspended the search for another day due to rough seas and the advancing storm.

Jamie watched Case pace the small confines of the cluttered store like a caged lion, wearing pathways in the old wooden planking.

"Damn." Case stopped pacing to look out the window. Outside the sky was getting grayer by the minute. They were running out of time and without more time, they would be going on a recovery mission instead of a search and rescue.

Even the seagulls were coming ashore. Another bad sign.

Jamie watched Shelby fiddle with the inventory, readjusting a stack of twine that needed no readjusting. It was busywork to keep her mind off of what was going on outside.

"I don't understand where that boy could be," Case growled. "I can't stand this. I don't care if they are calling off the search. I'm going to look for him myself. He's got to be out there somewhere."

"Uncle," Shelby yelled after him, but the door slammed behind him followed by a bang of a truck door and the starting whine of an engine. He could understand why Case was reacting the way he was. The worst part of a situation like this was the power of the unknown. Helplessness and fear conspire to make everything worse.

"I can't believe that he's going to risk his neck to go looking for Josh. It's bad enough that I may have lost my brother because of foolishness. He of all people should know better."

"Don't worry," Jamie said, moving to stand next to her and offering her a cup of the coffee he had just brewed. "Your uncle can take care of himself." The tension, worry and the coming storm were wearing heavy upon her. He looked at the deep lines etching her eyes and the sag of her shoulders.

"You really should try and get some sleep. There isn't anything that you can do for now. If you want, I can take care of the store for you." It was the least he could do.

She looked up at him with large eyes. "I can't do that to you. I can't just leave you with the whole store to run when you don't know anything about it. Besides, with so many of the fishermen in for the day and the storm coming, we are bound to be busy with people stocking up."

The bell above the door chimed as two old men walked into the store.

"Good morning John Henry. Roe, how are you today?" Two old men came in with gray hair and saggy work pants that were held up with red suspenders.

John Henry just nodded at her and went in search of the coffeepot, but Roe stopped to place a withered, work-roughened hand upon her arm. "How are you holdin' up, dear? I heard the news on the radio about them calling it off for the day."

It was the same two old men from Callaway's Pub. Jamie watched as Shelby did her best to smile at the gesture of kindness. She was doing her best to hold onto her hope, but he could see that her optimism was running out fast.

"I'm fine, really." But she wasn't. All night long he had lay in bed trying to go over everything that he had managed to find out so far, but his thoughts kept coming back to Shelby. It didn't take much to remember the heat of her fingers against his cheek and the honeyed smell of her, as she had stood so close.

He'd never met anyone quite like Shelby. But then, maybe he was wrong. Maybe he had met someone like her before. Her gentle manner and her ability to carry on through any crisis reminded him very much of his mother. Both women had a deep strength that came from within and both had suffered losses and had managed to persevere. Despite losing her son, his mother had rallied around her family, trying her best to pull together a family that was disintegrating before her eyes.

He had turned away from his mother because of the guilt and because he hadn't known how to comfort her. He was more like his father than he'd realized.

He watched Shelby for a moment as she placed a hand on the old fisherman's shoulder and bent over closer so she could hear his voice. She was so graceful in her gestures, so simplistic and genuine in her movements. She looked up and saw him watching her, offering him a small smile.

He was beginning to think and feel too much about Shelby. It had been a long time since he had stopped long enough to feel anything other than the simplest of emotions. Even when David had died he had only felt anger. He had never stopped to feel anything else.

There were ghosts here in Chandler that he had never wanted to face, ghosts of his own past that he saw when he looked at Shelby. What he needed was time and distance and to find the answers he needed. "I'm going down to the wharf to make sure that everything is secured down there."

And without waiting for a response he headed out the door.

Shelby watched as Jamie went out the door, pulling it closed behind him. The wind was picking up faster now, but the hurricane was stalled somewhere off of the coast of Cape Cod and Rhode Island. That meant that there was still some time left before the storm to get things settled, but the weather was a threatening reminder of what was to come. The cackling sounds on the radio had lessened as one by one the fishermen got their boats ready to ride out the storm and went in search of shelter.

She put her hands over the old woodstove in the corner and let the warmth sink into her fingers. She was just one big raw nerve. Waiting had never been her strong point and it hadn't changed much since Tommy's death, only gotten worse. The only thing she had to hold onto right now was that they hadn't found Josh's body. There was still a chance that he could be stranded out on one of the nearby islands. But as the time was passing it was getting harder to hold onto that hope.

She looked out the window and watched as Jamie made his way down the gravel pathway to the wharf. The sky was turning an odd gray cast and the morning sky held a hint of orange red fire.

"Red sky at night, sailors' delight. Red sky in morning, sailors take warning." She had heard those words all her life, but never had they been as ominous as they were at this moment. Her brother was somewhere out there, looking for shelter from the coming storm and probably blaming everyone else for his misfortune. He didn't have a clue how much chaos he had caused. And now, in desperation, her uncle had run off to look for him, leaving her behind to just wait and watch. If only there was something that she could do to help.

She watched as Jamie maneuvered along the flat sections of floating dock that were tied to the wharf. It rocked beneath his feet as water sloshed up and over the sides. He bent over to check a rope that was securing a wooden skiff. Having Jamie around had become a blessing, an unexpected comfort. She didn't know what she would have done without him here. He had arrived in Chandler a total stranger and yet, somehow she had come to rely on him as if she had known him all of her life.

She looked at Roe and John Henry huddled around the old barrel stove. They were the older generation, the ones that had never even left the security of Chandler. But what had she done with her life? She may have gone off to college to get her degree, but she had been pulled back here. There had never been a question of what she would do with her life. She had always just done the expected and when their father died, she had come back to run the business and to be close to her brother. She had never worried about making or having choices. There had never been any to make.

Marrying Tommy had also been a given. They had known each other all their lives and everyone had just assumed that they would end up together. In a very small amount of time they had gone from being friends, to dating, to being engaged, and then married. No one had ever questioned it. But now, here she was alone.

She looked once again out the window at Jamie. She had been wrong about him and while he had never set out to correct her impression of him, he had. Jamie Rivard was a good man. There was something about him that radiated strength. He had a nurturing spirit, though he didn't appear to want it. She had needed someone and he had come along at just the right time. Fate had sent a helping hand.

"Shelby, have you heard from Marianne today?" Roe said over the brim of his coffee mug. "John Henry and I went by her place this morning, but we didn't see any sign of her. Did she go somewhere to ride out the storm?"

"She should be there. She wouldn't go anywhere without at least letting me know." New worry filled her. It wasn't like Marianne to leave her house, especially if a storm was coming. Set up on the cliffs and in the stand of pines, her house was protected from the water and wind. "Maybe I should go check on her and make sure that she is okay."

The only problem was that her uncle had taken the truck. She looked out at Jamie. He was moving the lobster cars into the protection of the wharf pilings. Maybe he would take her to check on Marianne.

He had just finished tying up the last of the cars, when he caught sight of her making her way down the gravel path.

He moved back out onto the float to pick up a bucket when he noticed that she was hanging close to the shelter of the wharf. She could wait until he was done. He was trying to use this time to pull his thoughts together, but it was proving harder than he thought.

"Go back inside. I can finish this up. There's no sense in both of us being out here." He waved a hand at her, motioning her back to the shelter of the store.

He went back to picking up the loose buckets and ropes on the float. He stumbled a few times as the waves rocked the wood beneath him, bracing his feet against the movement; he bent over to retrieve another bucket and almost lost his balance all together when he felt a hand on his shoulder.

"What the . . ." A very white-faced Shelby gripped at his arm. "I told you to go back inside. I'll handle this out here. It's getting rough." He tried to shake off her grip, but stopped when she wouldn't let go. He looked again at her face and stopped. Sheer terror filled her gaze. Shelby was scared to death.

He pulled her to him, wrapping his arms around her. Her fingers grasped at his back, as she clung to him like a lost child. She buried her face against his chest. Her breath was warm against the coolness of his skin, a small whimper reverberating through her.

He had to get her out of there.

He half-pulled, half-carried the shaking Shelby up onto the dock and onto firm ground.

"What were you doing out there?" He grabbed her by the forearms and pulled her back from him. Her head was bent, her shoulders quaking. He put a hand under her chin, raising her gaze to his. Tears streamed down her cheeks leaving wet trails on her face.

"I tried to yell, but you couldn't hear me." Her words came out in small short gasps. "I'm so sorry. I just . . ." Her words trailed off and were caught by the wind. He put an arm around her and held her next to him as he walked back up the pathway to the store.

Once inside, he sat her down next to the

stove. Her hands were shaking, but her breathing had begun to ease up.

Roe set a cup of steaming coffee into her hands and motioned for her to drink it. "Are you all right, gal? What were you doing out there?"

He shook his head at Jamie. "I don't know why she'd do such a cussid, darned thing. She's downright scared of the water since Tommy died. Hasn't been out in a boat in a couple years." Even for all the harshness of his words, the old man settled a gentle hand upon her shaking shoulder.

"I'm so sorry." He had seen the terror in her eyes out there on that dock. He handed her a cup of coffee and she clutched it between her shaking fingers.

"I thought that I could go out there, but the waves are so rough. You couldn't hear me, so I moved a little bit at a time trying to get your attention." She shuddered. "I don't know what happened."

"I do. You're afraid of the water and you came out there anyway to get me." He moved to stand next to her. "What I don't understand is how you can run a business like this when you have a fear like that?"

Shelby shook her head. She was calmer now. "I wasn't always afraid of water. It's just been the last few years that I haven't been able to go out there. Not since Tommy died." The words were enough for him to understand the terror that he had seen on her face. Death had a way of placing unrealistic fears and expectations on a person. For Shelby, they had meant that she couldn't face the very thing that gave her a living.

"But if you can't go down there then how do you run the wharf business?"

She shrugged. "During the summer I hire a few of the local boys to help out. They do most of the work down there. What they can't do, my uncle has been doing." She got up to place her mug on the counter. She stood still, her back to him for a moment. He looked over at Roe and John Henry. Both old men where shaking their heads in concern.

"So, what was it that you needed so much that you were willing to come out there and get me?"

Shelby turned back from the counter. She was fast recovering. Her shoulders were straighter now and he could see again the gentle strength just below her surface.

"I need to go check on Marianne, but I can't get there in this weather without a ride. My uncle took the truck and I was wondering if you would take me out there?"

"You want me to take you out on my bike,

in this weather?" It would be a hard ride, with the wind picking up as it was. The late afternoon sky was already turning evening dark and there wasn't much time before the rains would start.

"Roe said that she wasn't there when they went to check on her and that has me worried. She depends on me and she rarely leaves the house." She looked up at him with her brown eyes and all of his arguments went out the window.

"Fine, we'll take my bike. It isn't the best weather for it, but it will have to do."

The wind whipped past her as she braced herself during the short walk from the bike to Marianne's house. It was an eerie time of dusk, when the stormy sky looked gunmetal gray and the ground was shadowed from the coming dark.

Rain pelted them, coming down in a torrent against the roof, reverberating like thunder as they ran for the house; the screen door screeching as she pulled it open and stepped into the shelter of the sleeping porch. The wind moved the screens back and forth with every gust. Jamie was behind her. Dark rivulets of moisture ran down his shirt leaving a dusky trail. Even with the effects of the storm-hindered trip, he was rather unnerving to look at. She chanced a look at his face. His eyes were shadowed, but she could feel his gaze on her. Quiet intensity radiated from him. How had she come to trust a man that she didn't know at all?

She pushed the hair out of her eyes and pulled her wet shirt away from the front of her. An uncontrollable shiver ran up her spine. Her nerves were raw and her stomach was sore from worry.

A light shone through the kitchen curtains. It was a welcome sight in such horrible weather. She reached for the handle only to find that the door was ajar. She swung it open the rest of the way and stepped into the small kitchen as Jamie followed behind her.

"Does she always leave her door open like that?" he asked.

"No. But she does get forgetful when she's painting." She stepped farther into the room and looked around. The cat's dish sat empty on the counter, the unopened cat food can beside it. "Marianne!" There was no response, only gusts of wind blowing the rain against the house and rattling the windowpanes.

Meribelle came from under the table to wind herself between Shelby's feet.

"Where's Marianne, girl?" But the cat only sat back on its rear quarter and stared up at her with wide eyes.

"Marianne?"

"Maybe she went out for a while."

Shelby looked out the window and the fast approaching storm. "She wouldn't have gone out in this. With her arthritis it would have been too difficult. She has to be around here somewhere." A million ideas began running through her mind. Maybe Marianne was hurt? Maybe she had fallen and struck her head? Maybe she couldn't call out to them for help?

She stepped into the darkened hallway. "Marianne, where are you?" The living room was as dark as the hallway. She walked toward the wide expanse of windows banking facing the ocean. Marianne's painting was still on the easel, unfinished, a brush set in the tray as though it had been discarded in haste.

"I don't like this. Something doesn't feel right." She turned to find Jamie looking out the window at the rain pelting the grass that edged downward to the cliffs and the water below.

"She has a great view here. I bet she sees everything." Jamie picked up the discarded binoculars on the windowsill as Shelby wrapped her arms around herself for warmth. She wasn't fighting just the chill of the rain-soaked clothes, but the feeling of dread that was fast filling her.

Jamie stopped in front of the painting, taking special interest in the wet paint that dotted the corner of the board. "Wherever Marianne is, she hasn't gone far. The paint is still wet on this part here by the boat house." She watched him squint harder at the corner that Marianne had been working on. Now was not the time for looking at paintings. Something in her gut was telling her that everything was not all right here.

"Marianne wouldn't have just walked off. She has to be here somewhere." Maybe she was upstairs. Marianne kept to the large living room, preferring to sleep on the couch downstairs rather than to make the painful climb. Shelby's foot had just hit the bottom step when Jamie's voice stopped her.

"Oh God!" He raced for the door, his footsteps clamoring against the wooden floor. She ran after him. Her heart was pounding in her ears; her mouth had gone dry.

She followed as best she could as his long legs jumped the few steps to the ground off the deck and ran toward the granite stairs leading down the cliff. The wind pushed at them like some maniacal hand sweeping them along and then pushing them back again. The trees bent as the wind drove through them, the sound echoing in her ears. It was as though she was on a merry-go-round that was tilting out of control. The rain had transformed the green grass into a slippery slide and she found herself colliding against Jamie's solid back as she skidded to a halt behind him. She was struggling to right herself when she felt his arm circle her, pulling her tight against him, and she pushed at him, determined to see what had made him stop. But he held her tight to him, his fingers cradling her head. Her wet hair slapped against her cheeks as the rain clung to her eyelashes making it difficult to see.

"Don't look, Shelby." She pushed at his hands until she could look over the side of the embankment. At first she couldn't see much. The wind and rain conspired together, creating a vacuum of sound and feel. Her body and brain were numb from the stinging of the rain and the onslaught of circumstances.

The low scrub pine edging the rocks looked like bony fingers twisting in the wind. Her gaze traveled downward, following the path of gray stones marking the steep cliffs until a small pinpoint of light caught her gaze. At first glance she dismissed it, an obvious trick of the storm. But then her gaze fell again on the light and the lighter gray of a sweater that covered an edge of a nearby rock. Bile filled her throat and she choked back the uprising in her chest. It was Marianne.

Jamie pulled her back again, steadying her, his body firm against hers. He reached up to pull her gaze back to his.

"Shelby." She could hear his voice saying her name above the whining of the wind, but the terror she felt had frozen her to her spot.

"Shelby, you've got to listen to me. I need to go down there, but I want you to stay here." Somehow she managed a nod.

She sank to her knees in the grass. Marianne was gone. She knew it, even before he reached her crumpled body. Marianne was gone and they were too late.

She watched in stunned silence as he bent, checking Marianne's lifeless body before straightening again. His head was down as he struggled back up the steps to where Shelby sat in the wet grass. He stood for a moment staring down at her, the line of his mouth grim and straight.

He bent down rocking on the heels of his

boots and resting his arms on his knees. She looked at the stiff set of his jaw and the white scar that stood out against his tanned skin.

He held out a hand to her and she took it, leaning heavily against him as she rose to her feet. She knew without a doubt at that moment, without any further words, that her flash of insight had been correct. Marianne was gone.

He pulled her once again into the tight circle of his arms. His hands came to rest one at her waist pulling her tight against him, the other at the back of her neck under the heavy folds of her wet hair.

She should be crying. But somehow she just felt numb. This must be shock, her mind reasoned. But her body was like a traitor refusing to move from the security of his embrace.

After a moment, she raised her face and found that Jamie's eyes were closed. He was pale. And then she felt a shudder run through him.

He opened his eyes and looked down at her. The slate gray of his eyes mirrored the intensity swirling around them, but she saw more there in the depths. Something she hadn't seen before.

"I'm sorry, Shelby." And she knew he

meant it.

She opened her mouth to respond, but the words were ripped from her with a blast. At first she would have sworn it was the wind, but within a second she found herself pinned to the ground. The cold grass matted beneath her and Jamie's body was heavy on top. She couldn't breathe. She couldn't think as another sound ripped past them and she realized that it wasn't the storm that had her in this position.

Someone was shooting at them.

This was another one of those coincidences that he hated so much. He would have bet his last dollar that someone had known that they were coming. Someone knew that they were going to show up at Marianne's. And whoever it was didn't believe in hand-to-hand. They were going straight for the heavy artillery.

The shooting stopped. At least for the moment. He couldn't hear anything above the wind. But if they had bothered to shoot at them, then they weren't afraid of coming up to the top of the cliff to see if they needed to finish the job.

Shelby struggled beneath him. He looked down at the top of her head. Her face was buried in the front of his jacket. He had to get her out of here.

Jamie scrambled off of her and she rolled into a crouch next to him.

"Who are they?" Her voice was a hoarse whisper. "Why are they shooting at us?"

"I wish I knew." He slid his arms out of his jacket and threw it over her shoulders.

Shelby stared down at his chest, her eyes wide and fixed. It was a moment before he realized that she was looking at the gun he'd kept in his shoulder harness. He didn't have time to explain. He didn't have time to explain anything at the moment and even if he did he didn't have a clue what he would say.

"I want you to stay low and go around to the back of the house and wait for me by the bike. I'll be there as soon as I can." He intended to find out who was shooting at them, but first he had to get her out of harm's way.

"But . . ."

"No buts. I need you to do this Shelby. Do what I ask and wait for me by the bike."

"But what about Marianne? We can't just leave her there. I can't just let her stay there." She started to stand and Jamie grabbed the back of the leather jacket, pulling her back down.

"We don't have any choice, Shelby. We'll

let someone know to come back for her, but right now we need to get you to safety." He gave her a push toward the direction of the back of the house. "Go! I'll be right behind you."

He watched her scramble off before disappearing behind the house. She should be safe for the moment by the bike. Whoever had shot at them was still close by the shoreline. The only way up the steep embankment was by the granite walkway. This meant that he should be able to see them coming.

He crawled on his stomach as close as he dared to the edge of the lawn and raised himself up until he could see. The water was whipping up, crashing with force against the black rocks. White caps filled the inlet.

Two figures were picking their way across the ledges, staying close to the ground. The meager light was not enough for him to get a good look at them. At least he could be sure that they would be far enough behind them that they could get a lead on them.

He was just about to turn away when he caught a splash of red against the angry sea. He hoisted himself up again as much as he dared, but the wind and rain and trees along the water edge were obscuring his view. It was a boat, but who would be crazy enough to be out on the water in a brewing hurricane?

Maybe someone who was crazy enough to kill an old woman and shoot at them.

A yell pierced through the wind's howl as they had spotted him. He scrambled backward half-crouching as he ran to catch up with Shelby.

She whirled around as he sprinted the last few feet to the bike, his feet slipping on the gravel that had turned to mud in the unpaved driveway.

He grabbed the helmet from the back of the bike and stuck it out in a wordless offering.

She stared at the helmet as though she had never seen it. Her eyes were open wide, her gaze haunting and hollow as the rain continued pouring down upon her. Her hair hung in wet rivulets about her pale face. She was beginning to show signs of shock and he didn't have time to do a damn thing about it.

"Take it!" He shouted against the roar of the rain and wind, but she still didn't move. "I said take it, you little fool." He stepped toward her, pushing the helmet onto her head and clasping it beneath her trembling chin.

He straddled the bike and then pulled her

on behind him. It could have been worse. She could be hysterical. He slipped the key in and turned over the engine, throttling the gas.

If they hadn't discovered where they had gone, they would once they heard the sound of the engine adding to the chaos of the storm. He could only hope and pray that they were far enough ahead to get a good distance between them.

Too bad he wasn't a man who prayed.

The wind whipped past them in a slash of stinging pellets. Each drop became a sharp pain, stinging her hands and face. Her jeans molded against her legs, stiffening the heavy fabric until she fought to bend with his body as he leaned into a curve.

She buried her head against the solid width of his shoulders. Her fingers splayed across the tense muscles that ran up his side. She squeezed her eyes shut, fighting the panic that was sitting solid like a rock in her stomach. The ringing in her ears rose against the thunderous noise of the bike's engine and her fingers tightened, gripping his sides as hard as she could to fight her rising fear.

Marianne was gone and her brother had disappeared. Neither of them deserved to have this happen to them. And now some-one was after them. Somehow her life had turned upside down and she didn't have a clue how to fix it.

Never had she imagined that she would end up racing through the night on the back of a motorcycle through a hurricane. Or, that she would trust her life to a man that she barely knew.

Correction, she knew *nothing* about Jamie. He had shown up like a knight in shining armor, racing to her rescue and pulling her from the edge of death. But the question still remained. How was it that the loner, who showed up looking for a job, carried around a gun and was capable of handling dangerous situations? Most men would have turned tail and run, leaving her to fend for herself. But Jamie had put his own life at risk by trying to help her.

Chapter Nine

This was the last place he'd ever expected to be again.

He locked the door behind them, setting the deadbolt with a loud click that echoed in the small entryway.

"What is this place?" Her quiet words held a hint of a shiver as she stood behind him in the doorway. He could see her small body outlined in the murkiness. She looked so small and defenseless, with her arms around herself beneath the generous folds of his jacket. He had to get her inside and warmed up very soon or she'd go into shock.

He ran his hand along the wall until he found the switch and flipped it. Nothing happened. The storm must have knocked out the power to most of the Maine coast.

"We should be safe here. The house has an alarm system that works on a backup battery system. It can run for hours without electricity." He punched some numbers on a control pad.

He had stashed the bike in the thick stand of trees on the road leading into the cottage and covered it with a black tarp for protection and to keep it from being noticed.

He raised a hand, sweeping back a strand of wet hair that hung in tangles about her stark, white face.

"Should we be in here?" Her voice was shaky.

"It's okay. I know the owners." He fumbled through the drawer of the cabinet by the door and pulled out a candle and a lighter. The small flame swept through the blackness, leaving the corners in the shadows. The room was paneled with painted beaded board, with a bench built along one wall. Jamie took her cold hand in his and led her through the doorway to a large room, using the candle to light the way.

She shivered under the heavy wet material of his jacket. Slipping the candle into a small vase that was set on a side table, he reached out to touch her hand. Her fingers were fragile icicles against his cold palm. She pulled her hand from his and clutched tighter at the zippered front of the leather coat. Her reactions were slow and muddled.

Shelby's eyes were like large shadowy pools in a stark white face. Jamie pulled her closer to him. The wet leather of his coat gave off an earthy scent as he unzipped the jacket and slid it from her shoulders. The slashing rain had permeated the lining and clung to her. He let the coat fall to the floor as her body swayed against him.

"Marianne is gone." She let out a soft cry as tears welled up and rolled down her cheeks. When he reached a hand up to brush away the tears, she closed her eyes, leaning her face against his hand. All the emotions, all the fear and all the loss was too much for her to keep inside any longer.

He needed to keep her safe.

Jamie pulled the dust cover off a nearby chair and guided her into it. He used the drop cloth to cover her up, tucking it around her shaking form. The fabric was thin, but it would help to give her back some much-needed warmth until he could find another way of supplying it. He looked around at the dark room. Right now he needed to investigate. From what he could tell they were alone, but he couldn't be sure until he checked it out for himself.

"Shelby, I need you to stay right here. Don't move unless I tell you it's safe."

She shook her head. "So pushy," she managed through clenched, chattering teeth.

"Just remember that and stay put. You'll

be all right here. I just need to go make sure that all of the doors and windows are secure."

She nodded.

He picked his way through the maze of covered furniture and checked all of the windows that lined the front wall of the house. On a sunny day, the view outside the windows was breathtaking. Tonight, the darkness outside the window held more mystery and danger than he really wanted to contemplate.

Convinced that the doors and windows of the living room were secure, he made his way toward the back of the house. The kitchen at Ledgeview was massive and old fashioned. Plain, tall cabinets reached to the full height of the ten-foot tin ceilings and his sneakers squeaked on the linoleum tile. He checked the windows and the back door and found that all was secured. The only thing left to check was the second floor, but someone would have to be an idiot to try and scale the height in all the wind the storm was generating.

Outside the sound of the shutter rattling clattered like stones against the glass. The storm was picking up in intensity. They had gotten to Ledgeview just in time. A few more minutes out in the storm and they wouldn't have been able to control the bike on the slick roads.

He fumbled his way through the kitchen, guiding himself by memory. The only light was the occasional illumination from the lightning flashing outside.

Just off the kitchen was a small shed. He unlocked the door and stepped down the two steps that took him to the bare concrete floor. It wasn't much, just an uninsulated space used to store gardening tools and the lawnmower. The stale scent of old dirt and dampness wafted to him as he made his way through the small room. In the corner he uncovered a small stack of wood. The rotted and crumbling pieces fell apart when he tried to lift them. But it was enough to get a fire going so they could warm up. The coarse wood pricked his cold fingers. What he wanted right now, more than anything, was a hot shower but that wasn't likely to happen anytime soon.

Taking care, he gathered an armload of the firewood, piling some of the bigger pieces together until he had enough for a fire and then made his way back through the kitchen and into the living room. Shelby had cast off her wet sneakers and socks and pulled her feet up under her and the blanket. She shivered, a ripple passing through her before she snuggled further into the flimsy fabric.

"I found some wood. I'll have a fire going in no time."

She nodded at him. Her wide eyes followed his movements as he set about laying the fire. He pulled some old newspaper out of a nearby box and stuffed it between the old logs, touching the flame of the lighter to the logs, he watched the dry wood explode with the heat.

Jamie slipped off his shoulder holster and set it on a side table before peeling off his own wet shirt and spreading it out onto the flagstone surround of the fireplace. Shelby continued to stare into the fire. Uncontrollable tremors racked her body, jolting her beneath the thin sheet. He needed to get her warmed up.

Grabbing the arms of the chair, he dragged it closer to the fire. She looked up at him and blinked. "Thank you." Her small words were enough to reassure him, but he still needed to convince himself that she was going to be okay. The sooner he got her dry and warm, the faster she would be able to handle whatever was ahead of them.

She protested as he pulled the sheet off of her. He pulled her to her feet in front of the fire and wrapped an arm around her to keep her steady. He pulled the wet fabric of her shirt free from her soaked jeans and threw it down onto the hearth next to his own. He rubbed his hands up and down her arms, as he tried to bring the warmth back to her body. She shook as the cold air touched her wet skin. The thin fabric of her bra was transparent and flimsy against the effects of the cold. She fought against his hands.

"What are you doing?" Her angry words came out as a strangled gasp as he pulled her closer against him and set to work one-handed on the button of her jeans.

"I'm only warming you up." Under better circumstances the sight of Shelby standing before him, clad only in half-undone jeans and a pale pink lace bra that reminded him of the color of cotton candy and hot afternoons, would have caused enough heat in him to fill the old house. He swallowed hard against the lump in his throat. Right now he needed to focus on getting her dried off, warm and safe.

"Don't." The words were growled between her chattering teeth. He worked harder on the zipper of her jeans. Her cold palms pressed against his chest. Her fingers splayed against him and he willed his body not to react. Now was not the time to indulge in fantasies, no matter who inspired them.

"I'm sorry to do this to you, Shelby. But if I don't get you out of these wet clothes you're going to end up sick. And I don't want you to get sick. It's nothing personal." But it was fast becoming personal to him. It was hard to ignore the attraction coursing through him when he was near her.

He pried down the rest of her zipper and moved to slide them down her legs, pale and translucent in the firelight. Only a scrap of pale blue lace covered the rounded curve of her bottom and her delicate womanly V. The high rounded legs and low waist fit Shelby like the molded leather seat in a fine Italian sports car.

Now was not the time, he reminded himself again.

"Thank you." She was chattering less now. The involuntary shudders had lessened. He sat her down in front of the fire and wrapped the sheet around her again. She closed her eyes as the heat of the fire seeped into her.

"I don't think I have ever been so cold." Her voice was small. He grabbed another sheet off a nearby chair and shook the dust from it before using the edge to rub her wet hair. She pulled her knees up and rested her chin on them, keeping her back to the fire and Jamie.

Her shivering lessened until it was just an occasional quiver. She turned to face him and opened her eyes. Gone was the wide-eyed look of fear. She gave him a small weak smile. "You must be frozen."

Jamie shrugged and continued to use the cloth on her hair. He was hot enough sitting next to her. She was having a warming effect on all of his senses. "Cold doesn't bother me too much. I spent some time in Alaska a couple of years ago, so being in Maine during a hurricane is nothing."

The sounds of the fire crackling helped to muffle the roar of the elements outside. She looked at the blackness outside the windows. How had she ended up here? How could she have gotten to this point? Her brain was still fuzzy from the numbing wet cold, but a few things still registered. Her brother had disappeared, Marianne was dead and someone was now after Jamie and her. How had her life gotten to this point? She was just a simple woman who had lost her husband and had managed to eke out a life for herself. She was happy running a family business and living in the house she had grown up in. She was happy with her life. So why was it that once again fate had chosen to throw a monkey wrench into her mild mannered life?

She watched Jamie get up from his place near the fire. He opened a cabinet near the window and started rummaging through, searching for something.

"Are you sure the owners won't mind us being here?"

"They won't mind." His response was muffled as he dug further into the far corner of the cabinet. "Aha! I knew there had to be one in here somewhere." He pulled out a flashlight and tested the switch. "It's not the greatest, but it should be enough to help." He strode back toward her, flashlight in hand. She watched the light of the fireplace flicker across his chest. It was the first time she had seen him without a shirt on. The orange and yellow flames deepened the dark lines of his body. A trail of coarse dark hair trailed down in a narrow line before disappearing below the waistband of his jeans.

"We should be safe enough here. This place belongs to my family."

Her gaze shot back to his face. "I thought you said that you were from New Orleans?"

"I am. This is our summer home. It's been in the family for over a hundred years. My great-grandfather built it for his wife as a way to escape the heat of New Orleans summers." He scooted down next to her, flashlight in hand. His smile was the same masking one he had given her before.

"My parents used to come every summer until my father got sick." He laid a hand against her cheek. "Are you sure you are feeling okay? Your fingers and toes aren't hurting are they?" He reached for the fingers she had curled around the edge of the sheet. Her skin tingled as he ran his hands over hers, holding them up to the light of the fire. "They look fine."

His touch burned her skin. She pulled from his grasp and clasped the blanket tighter around herself.

"I'm fine, really."

He looked at her for a moment. His gaze driving into her as though trying to discover what was beneath her skin. With his hair slicked back and the light of the fire behind him, the whitened ridge of the scar above his eye looked more pronounced. She put a finger up tracing the length of it before he reached out stilling her action.

"How did you get it? The scar can't be that old." He pulled away at her words, not physically, but mentally. Gone was the intent introspective gleam. She had gone too far. She had crossed that invisible line he'd drawn for himself. Back again was the wall that protected him.

He let out a small laugh. "I guess you could say that I'm a real klutz. I fell down and gashed it open. It was nothing." There was a smile on his face, but it didn't quite reach his eyes. He got up and held out a hand to her, pulling her to her feet. She held the drop cloth tight. The length of it pooled around her feet. Knowing that she must look ridiculous after their wild ride in the rain, she put a hand up to her hair. It was drying from the heat of the fire, but she didn't need a mirror to tell her that it must be sticking out all over.

"You look beautiful." He laughed at her self-conscious gesture. "Only a woman would be concerned about how she looked after what we've been through tonight." His words were meant to be a joke, but the reality was that someone was after them and that was enough to put some of the chill back into the air for her. She hugged the sheet tighter around her.

"You think I look beautiful?" She couldn't help the words that tumbled out of her. It had been a long, long time since someone had called her beautiful.

His gaze was intense and his jaw set, when he responded.

"Yes, I do." It appeared to be a struggle for him. But why she didn't know. Maybe he was fighting this attraction between them for a very good reason. He could have a girlfriend or even a wife somewhere for all she knew. And maybe he was just humoring her to keep her from going into shock.

He steered her in the direction of the stairs with a gentle hand at the base of her back. The warmth of his touch burned her skin through the fabric of the sheet, warming her inside. With one simple touch he had managed to make her feel safer than she had in a very long time. She stepped onto the bottom step and turned to face him. She wanted to say thank you, but she wasn't quite sure how she could ever thank him for what he was doing for her. But her words stilled on her lips. The height of the step had brought her gaze level with his. Stormy intensity radiated from his gaze as he stared back at her. The light from the fire increased their brilliance.

Her gaze shifted downward to his lips. Gone was the wry aloof smile she had seen so many times. The soft sensuous curve of his lips was set in a grim, tight line. She wanted to kiss him. Maybe it was all they had been through, or maybe she'd just been alone too long. But just this once she wanted to take a chance.

She closed the small intimate distance between them; her eyes drifting shut as she brushed her mouth soft against his closed lips.

He stood still and for a moment she thought she had misread the growing attraction she had felt. She thought she would be the fool. But a low sound erupted in his chest and traveled upward. His hands came up to frame her face, his fingers cupping her jaw.

All her guesses flew away as his mouth settled against hers. He blew gentle kisses against the outline of her closed lips; butterfly soft touches that made her melt against him. He growled again as her hands moved down his body, encircling his waist and settling against the bare sensitive skin edging the waistband of his jeans.

She opened her mouth to his, welcoming him as she pulled him even closer. His hands traveled downward to settle soft against her upper arms. His grip was firm, but gentle. Soft, but possessive.

Her body reacted through the thin fabric of the sheet and her bra. She wanted to touch him and she wanted him to touch her.

His tongue met hers, dancing, mating, matching and powerful. She responded. Her body giving as good as she received.

And then he pulled back, resting his forehead against hers. She kept her eyes closed, unwilling and unable to stop the surge of power coursing through her. She felt wanton and needed. She was feeling more than she had in a very long time. She felt like a woman again.

"Wow." Her words came out as a harsh whisper. She pulled back and dared to open her eyes. His expression was dark, soft and teasing. He smiled just a little and this time it went all the way to his eyes.

"Wow, is right." His own voice was unsteady and raspy. He fingered the line of her jaw before dropping his hands to her waist. "You are a dangerous lady." His words served to bring back the seriousness of their situation. For one endless minute they had forgotten the hellish ride, the rain, her brother's disappearance and Marianne.

"I'm going to take the flashlight and see if I can get the old generator in the shed going. I know it's dark, but if you go up the stairs you should be able to find some clothes to warm you up." His finger came up to trace the edge of the sheet where it slid from her shoulder. "Not that I don't like this look on you, but I think you might be more comfortable in something else."

The teasing sound was back in his voice and she smiled just a little.

"I don't think that this is the latest in fashion. Maybe something else would be better," she said, looking into those eyes that appeared even darker than the storm outside. He was a man who had too many mysteries. The biggest mystery was the man, himself. On the outside he alternated between casual, languid confidence and masking indifference. But she suspected that there was much more to Jamie Rivard's true self.

On impulse, she leaned forward and brushed her lips against his cheek. She needed to touch him one last time to reassure herself that what had happened, had happened. He turned, bending toward her touch. The man was not quite as indifferent as he would like to appear. Tonight, he had become her protector, her knight in shining armor, racing to save her.

His voice was soft and low and close in her ear. "Try the top of the stairs. It's my parents' room. There should be some clothes in there that will fit you." He turned her back toward the stairs and gave her another gentle push to guide her. She could feel the heat of his gaze following her up and into the darkness.

■ ■ ■ ■

Jamie watched the gentle sway of her backside as she stepped barefoot up the stairs and into the darkness beyond. The way that woman walked should be a crime and the most sensual part about it was that he was sure she didn't have a clue that just watching her walk could make him hot.

He turned and headed away from Shelby and the direction of his thoughts, making his way back toward the kitchen shed and the old generator. He should have given her the flashlight, but it was needed to see his way to fixing the old machine. With a little luck, they would have some power before long and then they could focus on figuring out what their next step would be.

In the old shed the walls were paper-thin to the outside. The storm sounded much louder and closer than it had before.

Jamie picked his way around the piles of discarded tools and equipment to the corner where the generator sat, covered with a tarp. Pulling the tarp off, he eyed the old machinery. It hadn't been used in the ten years since the family had last come to Ledgeview. There hadn't been any need for it since that summer when it had all happened.

He pushed the invading thoughts from his mind, not ready or willing to face the past. Now was not the time. But once again fate was playing a hand in bringing him to Ledgeview. He had intended to never come, but with those men on their tails they had needed someplace safe to stay and there wasn't any safer place than here.

He reached over, choking the engine and pulling the handle a few times. The generator gave a wizened cough and sputtered more. He gave it a few more tries before it roared to life with a moaning hesitation. It wasn't much, but it would give them some much-needed light.

The image of her face floated into his mind, the way the firelight played against her skin and how soft her touch had been. But Shelby wasn't the type that would be happy with a man who was always moving and she wouldn't be happy with just a casual affair. She was a forever kind of woman, the kind he had always avoided. Until now.

He was only certain of one thing about Shelby at this point. She was no longer a suspect and it wasn't because she had kissed him. It was clear that whoever had been shooting at them today had not considered her a friend. They wanted them out of

Chandler. She was one person off his list of suspects. The only problem was that he still had a long list of other people and he didn't have a clue as to how the ammunition fit into it all.

Shelby reached a hand into the dresser drawer and her fingers brushed against a soft, worn, terry fabric. She pulled it out and held it to the almost nonexistent light coming through the window. Outside the storm appeared to have stalled above them. The wind and rain swirled about the house as if it were in the vortex of the storm with no calming eye, only chaos. Lightning flashed through the lace curtains and she saw that she held a pair of elastic cuffed pants. She laid them over her arm and opened another drawer. This time she pulled out a worn-washed denim shirt. The soft fabric was like a welcoming blanket. She slipped on the shirt and pants and reveled in the warmth they offered. She rummaged around again until she found a pair of cotton socks and she slipped them on, wriggling her toes, warmth seeping into her bones, replacing the cold and wet.

She had kissed Jamie. She had never been so bold. It wasn't her way to be bold. She was steady and reliable and always did the right thing. She couldn't remember ever having initiated a kiss in her life. But then, she had never had a kiss quite like the one they had shared.

Her attraction to Jamie was bigger than any she had ever experienced. Maybe she had just been alone too long. Maybe her soul was telling her that it was time to take a chance again. But was he the right one to take a chance with?

Jamie was an unknown. Everything about the man was a mystery. This house spoke of old money and elegance and yet, she had labeled him a drifter, a wanderer. He had a past that for some reason he was running from. She wasn't sure that she wanted to be the one to uncover his secrets.

She was just about to head out of the bedroom when she heard the wheezing and whining of the generator powering up. Out of curiosity, she put a hand to the light switch by the door and flipped it on, illuminating the room. Outside the storm still raged, but from the dim light of the antique fixtures she could see that years of love and attention had made this place a wonderful home. For a master suite it was small. There was barely room for the large brass bed, dresser and an antique armoire, but she could see why it was so special. The room was like stepping into the past. The only light came from the spindly fixture that hung from a medallion in the center of the ceiling. The walls were decorated with large pink cabbage roses, and a white chenille bedspread covered the high bed and matched the fringe on the pillow shams. It had a cottage feel to it, not at all the posh summer home look that she had expected.

She was just about to shut out the light and make her way downstairs when a display of photos covering the dresser top caught her attention.

She picked up the smallest one, holding it up to the light. Two young boys stood together near the water, their arms draped around each other and their faces alight with an infectious grin. The older boy had blond hair and freckles. His skinny knees poked out from beneath baggy shorts. The younger of the two was darker. He stood straighter, stiffer, staring into the camera lens. Everything about the boy was intense. His gaze was more piercing, his smile brighter. It had to be Jamie. Even as a child Jamie had been dark and intense. But who was the other boy?

Her gaze traveled onward to the most ornate of the frames. The guilt edges and intricate Victorian design were a perfect setting for the hand-colored wedding portrait. The bride was dressed in fanciful lace that brushed the edges of her swan-like neck as she gazed upward at the man next to her. The groom was as dark as she was pale. His eyes were the same dark intense color, his nose the same aquiline shape as the man downstairs. This could only be Jamie's mother and father. It was easy to see where Jamie got his good looks.

She set the picture down and looked at the last frame. It was taller than the rest, hidden by the others. She was about to pass it over when something made her stop and look closer. She pulled it out staring at the photo of Jamie. Here was the same intense, half-smiling, half-knowing look she had become familiar with. Only this time his worn jeans and fitted shirts had been replaced with a uniform. A United States Coast Guard uniform.

"We have another problem," Caruso said. There was silence on the other end for a long moment. The storm made the line crackle and hum until it was almost drowned out by the roar of the wind outside.

"What do you mean we have a problem? I thought I told you to take care of it?" The old man's voice carried through the line.

"We've lost part of the shipment. We've only recovered two of the boxes. The third one disappeared." Caruso winced at the sharp curse that came across the line. They had screwed up this time. But then it wasn't their fault.

"How the hell did you let that happen?"

Caruso cringed as another gust of wind reverberated across the phone line. He didn't know which was worse, waiting for all hell to break lose, or trying to explain to the old man how they had screwed up.

"We've got a hurricane going on up here, damn it. We aren't in a position to be able to go looking for the other box. With the storm surge that package could be anywhere from here to Cape Cod and we'd end up drowned, while looking for it."

"I don't care," the boss said and Caruso believed him. "I want you to find that last box. It's my butt on the line here. I'm the one that they're going to come to looking for answers if this whole thing blows up. I can't risk a mistake. I won't tolerate it. I want you to find the package now."

Caruso hesitated for a moment, gauging his words. What he had to say wasn't going to help their situation. The old man was an idiot. He wasn't about to risk his neck searching for something that was most likely sunk to the bottom of the ocean. If his own neck weren't on the line, he would have told him where to put the box.

"I think that we should pull out now. We have enough. Things are getting too involved here."

"What do you mean 'too involved'? I'm counting on you to handle this with discretion. I can't risk having anyone uncovering this operation."

"I'm saying that I think we should cut our losses and pull out of here. People are starting to get suspicious. We had a problem with one of the locals that we had to take care of tonight."

"Was it Rivard?"

"No, a woman who was watching us." There was a not-so-muffled curse on the other end of the line.

"I asked you to do something simple. Rivard shouldn't have been that hard to handle, but you couldn't even do that without messing up. I want Rivard out of the picture and I want it done now. Can you do that?" Anger permeated the phone line.

Caruso sighed. He was going to have to tell him sooner or later. "Rivard disappeared and he took that Teague woman with him. We lost track of them at the old woman's house."

The old man let out another string of curses. "You're both idiots. I'm going to have to pull my contact out and let them know that there won't be any more shipments. They're not going to be happy about this and these are not people that you want to make mad."

"Do you still want us to go after Rivard?" Right now, the only thing Caruso wanted to do was find a safe place to hunker down for a while.

There was a rustle of paper on the other end of the line. "Here it is. I knew this would come in handy. He's got to be there."

Caruso was as confused as ever. "You know where Rivard is?"

"I know better than you do where he is and I'm not even there. Go look for him at a place called Ledgeview. It's his family's home on Crater Point. If Rivard's looking for a place to hide out with that woman, then he's probably gone there."

There was another moment of silence. "I am expecting it to be done right this time. If you can't handle it, then I'm going to have to come up there and handle it myself."

The line went dead.

Chapter Ten

Her sock-covered feet made almost no sound on the smooth wood as she made her way down the stairs. Jamie was perched on the wide flagstone hearth, pitching pieces of the dry wood into the fire.

"I see you found something to put on."

Shelby nodded, but didn't say anything as she made her way toward the warmth coming from the fireplace.

"I left the lights off. I don't know how long the storm will last or the generator will keep running, but it's best to conserve the power as much as we can." Firelight glinted off his bare chest. His dark hair was almost dry now, curling wildly about his neck.

"Are you hungry? I found some candy bars in my saddlebag. It isn't much, but it's enough to get us by for a while." He reached out a hand to pass her a candy bar and she stared at it a moment before taking it.

"You're prepared for anything, aren't

you?" she said.

"Well, I try." He unwrapped the candy bar and bit into it, then set it aside. "I have a sweet-tooth. Aren't you hungry?" he said, motioning at the unwrapped candy bar she held.

Shelby shook her head. "I'm fine, just a bit confused at the moment."

The last few days had rushed by in a blur and suddenly she realized that she was stranded in a house with a man she barely knew, someone who was other than what he had led her to believe. She was feeling betrayed. For the first time in ages she had put herself out, letting someone get close. Even daring to take a step toward intimacy, and it was all based on a deception.

She looked at the handgun he had set on the side table. The holster was soft leather, worn with use. Jamie Rivard had a past he was determined to conceal. Things were beginning to make sense to her that she had never thought to question before. Now, she understood how he had been able to take command of the situation when her brother had turned up missing. He'd known exactly what to do while she'd been paralyzed by fear because that was what he was trained to do.

But questions remained. Was he still in

the Coast Guard? And if so, then what was he doing in Chandler pretending to be a drifter without a past?

Jamie got to his feet. "Why don't I see if I can scrounge up something to drink?"

She watched him retreat into the darkness of the kitchen then moved to the bookcases lining the wall near the stairs. There was everything from first editions to paperback romances stuffed within the shelves. Here and there, someone had placed a shell or a piece of driftwood, sentimental reminders of a day outing or some memory they wished to cherish.

She felt, rather than heard, him return. She turned to find that he had stopped just a few steps behind her, watching her.

"This is quite an impressive collection." She picked up a first edition Hemingway and fingered the binding. Placing it back on the shelf, she moved onto the next bookcase. Again, there were a hodgepodge of interests, books about Maine, books on gardening, and several on sailing. There were even a few about law. She picked up a leather bound volume and looked at the cover. It was written by Theodosius Rivard.

"It's one of my father's books. He's a judge in New Orleans, a real old time politicking lawyer. When I was a little boy we would come for a couple of months during the summer and he used to write nonstop, when he wasn't sailing."

"You must have loved coming here. It's a wonderful house." She moved on down the length of the bookcase, trailing a finger along the shelves until she came to one that was filled with seashells and sea glass.

"What is this?" She picked up a small round stone from a shelf. The smooth black object was cool beneath her fingertips as she ran her hand over it.

"It's obsidian. My father brought it back to me from Hawaii."

"Obsidian? I've never heard of it." He took the paperweight from her and held it up to the light from the fireplace. A smile curved at his lips, but it was a smile that held a hint of regret.

His voice was rough, lending a graveled edge to his southern lilt. "I'd forgotten about this."

"I loved rocks when I was a kid. I read everything that I could get my hands on about them and how they're formed." He smiled. "This kind is formed when hot lava cools fast. It leaves behind a deep black stone." He let out a soft chuckle. "But this was extra special to me because of my father. I carried it around for weeks, after he brought it home. I was sure that it was magical and it would enable me with mystical powers that would somehow turn me into a true hero, like some knight of the round table."

"You must miss your father very much. It's so hard when you lose someone you are so close to."

Jamie stiffened, the smile disappearing from his face. She had gone too far, overstepping an invisible boundary that Jamie kept. She suddenly realized that in the time they had been together he had barely mentioned his family.

"My father is still alive." His voice held a quiet edge. "He and my mother still live in New Orleans." He looked down at the rock, but she knew he wasn't actually seeing it. "I talk with my mother once in a while on the phone, but I haven't seen them for quite some time."

She reached out, placing her hand over his, her fingers twining with his and curling around the stone. This time when they touched the piece of obsidian, it emanated warmth instead of cold, taking on the heat from his touch.

Jamie turned his hand, entwining his fingers with hers; the stone still locked between them. His eyes had taken on a black hue in the light of the fire. They held a depth and translucent aura of mysticism. Her breath caught within her. He looked so vulnerable, so much like a lost little boy.

She was becoming too attached to him. Every little bit of him that he let her glimpse made her feel closer to him. She knew she should turn away from him, but she was held by the look in his eyes.

"Perhaps, it does have magical powers, after all."

Every nerve ending in her body sprang to life with his gentle words. The room was warmer now and the flickering light of the candles shut out the last of the harsh experiences of the day. For a moment she could believe that it was just any other ordinary day and that he was an ordinary man who just happened to be interested in her.

He raised their intertwined fingers to his mouth. His soft lips grazed the ridge of her knuckles, sending a shiver up her back that settled at the base of her neck. She had no power to move and no power to speak, only to feel. He slipped his fingers from hers and turned her hand upward, her palm open to his ministrations. She watched in silent fascination as his lips parted and his tongue danced out to taste the skin upon her wrist.

She was entranced. Soon she would be a

puddle of water at his feet. Her knees already quivered and her stomach was contracting as she fought the surge of energy rushing through her.

Outside the walls, the storm swirled around them, and, inside, desire danced within her at his gentle touch.

"You have a power over me that I don't quite understand. In the short time that I've known you, you have made me feel and remember things that I haven't felt in years. Things I haven't wanted to remember. How is it that you can do that to me? I don't even know you."

Her sigh was his answer. A gentle whoosh of air escaped her parted lips. Her gaze entranced him. Her eyes were pools of sea-green water swirling in a tossing ocean. Jamie suppressed the urge to reach up and touch her hair where it brushed the curve of her shoulder.

Shelby was like no other woman he had ever met. For once he let himself look beyond the outside exterior of a woman and enjoy the strength beneath. She had all the qualities he had never let himself think of wanting, a heart full of caring, strength that came from deep inside, and a loyalty to the people who mattered most to her.

She reached her free hand up to touch his forehead, letting her fingers trail downward across the raised edge of the scar above his eye to the rough darkened stubble on his jaw. The tracing of her finger left a trail of heat against his skin. He wanted more. The realization startled him. He had desired women before, but it had never been with the consuming power that he felt at Shelby's touch. He grasped her fingers, stilling her gentle exploration.

"It's my turn to be self-conscious. I must look pretty horrible, with all of this running from danger."

His words broke the quiet tenuous bond between them and reality seeped in to intrude. He needed distance from her. When he was this close, it was hard to think.

Jamie pulled away from her. He couldn't look at her face. He didn't want to see the confusion he knew would be there. Instead, he focused on the stone she still had in her hands. He took it from her and turned back to the bookcase, placing it on the shelf.

Inside, he was cursing himself, calling himself every name he knew, and he knew quite a few. He was a fool. With one kiss, he had managed to forget every reason he had for being there. When he held her, he forgot that he was in Chandler to solve a case and when he looked at her he forgot that their lives were in danger. Being with Shelby, being this close, he had pushed aside all of his training and forgotten to remain distanced and unaffected.

It wasn't going to be easy to separate himself from the attraction that he was feeling for her. Right now, the only thing he was sure of was that he had to find a way to keep some space between them.

Someone out there wanted them dead. Their lives were on the line and he was more determined than ever to get them out of it. He needed to keep her safe. He couldn't think about what would happen if he failed. He just didn't know yet how he was going to do it.

"You know, I think that you owe me some answers, Jamie. I've chosen to trust you because of how you have helped my family and me. But I deserve to know the truth about who you really are, and why you're in Chandler. I know that you didn't just happen to come here out of the blue." She had moved to the window, watching the play of the rain against the panes of glass. It was impossible to see anything beyond their small world inside the house.

He knew that he owed her explanations. He could no longer put her in the middle of something so dangerous without letting her know the score.

"I don't know where to begin. It isn't that easy to tell." He ran a tired hand through his hair.

"You can start with who you really are and then tell me why those men killed Marianne," she said.

He had to tell her the truth, even if it was going to blow his cover. Right now, Shelby was the only person he could trust. As for the questions, he wasn't sure if he had any answers for himself.

He motioned for her to sit and she lowered herself onto the covered couch. She looked small and pale against the white dust cover.

If he told her everything then he ran the risk of scaring her, of having her leave, and right now he wasn't willing to accept that. Whoever it was that had seen them at Marianne's this evening wasn't about to stop until they had found a way to keep them quiet.

He settled back against the chair and stared into the orange flames of the fire. "This isn't easy. It's not all cut and dried. There are things that I can't tell you. There are things that I don't have answers to myself, yet."

She let out a heavy sigh. "You're talking

in circles, Jamie. Either you can't tell me, or you won't. Which is it?"

He could understand her frustration. He was fighting himself for the same answers. Whether he liked it or not, Shelby had become important to him. More than anyone had in a very long time.

Chapter Eleven

It was tearing him up inside. Giving himself up to the temptation of kissing her had somehow broken something loose within him. She had him thinking about things that were long in the past. The very essence of the power pulling them together had him confused and heated. She had become a part of him, in the short turbulent time that he had known her.

"This isn't easy for me. You're going to have to trust me on this."

"Oh." Her words were small and just the barest of a whisper that hung between them. He was asking her to put her faith in him, when he wasn't quite sure of himself. Right now, he needed her behind him. He needed to know that she would believe that he could get them out of this mess. And all of a sudden, her faith in him mattered as much as solving this case for David.

"You aren't just a wanderer, are you?

You're in Chandler for a reason."

He shook his head. "No, though my family would tell you that I've spent a good deal of my life running away from things." Things like life, pasts, and relationships.

"Is that why you joined the Coast Guard? So you could escape from things?" He looked up in surprise. She tried a casual shrug, but he could see that it wasn't such an easy question to put off. "It wasn't hard to figure out when I saw your picture on the dresser upstairs. The uniform was a dead giveaway."

"I came here to find some answers. I need your help to get to the bottom of this."

"Well, you have it. I don't know why, but you do." She let out a resigned sigh. "I'll help you, however I can. What is it that you need to know?"

It had been a long night and getting longer still. He wasn't sure if he had the energy to take this slow, without scaring her.

"When we were at Marianne's that first day I saw a pair of binoculars on the windowsill. Yesterday, she had them with her when I found her body. She was watching something or someone. Had she mentioned anything to you about activity in the area?"

"She did mention that there had been a lot of boat activity around the point, when we were there the other day. I didn't think too much about it at the time. There are always plenty of boats in the area, working, or pleasure wise, one or two more wouldn't make that much of a difference —" she said, hesitating as she looked out the window for a moment.

"But you've seen something. Haven't you?"

She turned back from the window, looking at him with wide eyes. She nodded.

"When I was at the point the other day I saw a plane coming in low over the cove. It was late and I couldn't make out much in the dark, but when it circled over the point it dropped something out. I searched the rocks as best I could, but I didn't find anything. So I decided to go back the next day and see if I could figure out what it was."

"And you didn't find anything?"

Again, she shook her head. "I went back the next night to see if it would happen again. The plane did come back. It circled the cove and then headed back out to sea just as it did the first time, but this time it didn't appear to drop anything."

"So, you've seen it twice and each time the plane flew over the cove it went back out over the ocean instead of the land? Do you have any idea what kind of plane it was?"

"I don't know. I don't know anything about planes and it was dark. It was small, not much bigger than one of those seaplanes that I see once in a while. But in the dark it was impossible to make out any kind of markings or distinguishing features."

They were making their drops by plane. That was a piece of the puzzle that he hadn't counted on.

And if the smugglers were local, then his original suspicions were correct. The guns could be moving in and out of Chandler, without being noticed. They could be going out of the harbor by truck or they could be picked up by local boats and transported to another area or to a waiting vessel for transportation. But where, and when?

If they were being transported by boat then that would explain what Taimon and Caruso were doing sitting off the coast. Transporting stolen items was their specialty.

The part that had him confused him the most, though, was why they had chosen to involve locals. Taimon and Caruso weren't the type to give locals or anyone a cut in their operations. They were more likely to keep the whole thing to themselves with outside involvement to a minimum. Maybe Josh wasn't involved in the trafficking; maybe he had stumbled onto what they were doing? He hoped for Josh's sake that he was wrong and her brother had just found a place to weather out the storm.

"Why are you in Chandler, Jamie? Because you aren't here to work on my uncle's lobster boat."

Jamie shook his head. He didn't know how else to break it to her. It wasn't so easy to explain. After everything that he was finding out, he wasn't so sure himself, what his role was for being here. But Shelby deserved an answer.

"I'm a Special Investigative Officer for the U.S. Coast Guard, and I was sent to Chandler to investigate the smuggling activity in the area because of my familiarity with the area."

She came and sat down next to him, on the arm of the chair. She put a hand on his and the warmth touched his heart.

"So they sent you in to bust whoever is behind the smuggling? But I thought that they did this kind of thing all the time. What is the difference between this and what they usually handle?"

Good question. He wasn't quite sure of the answer himself. The answer had to be in the supposed inside connection. That gave him one more reason not to trust too much.

"Three months ago one of our officers found a connection between some guns that were traced through a Florida pawn shop and showing up in Maine. A couple of days ago I found a package of guns out at the point tied to a trap line that had been cut. From what I have been able to piece together, I believe that the plane that you were talking about is dropping the smuggled guns and they're being picked up, by a contact in a boat. My information suggests that they are smuggling them into Northern Ireland."

"Into Northern Ireland. But why?"

"Guns are big business to the terrorist factions in Northern Ireland right now. I would say that they're selling them off to the highest bidder."

He watched her take in the information. For someone who had been through so much, it was amazing to him that she was handling it all so well. He dealt with this on a regular basis and at times it still shook him up.

"But, I still don't understand why they would need to call you in when there are Coast Guard stations all along the Maine coast."

Jamie got to his feet and paced to the

bookcase, then back again. He'd never had to explain to anyone, about what he did. It wasn't the kind of job that you talked about. He kept a low profile. Everything had always been the way that he liked it, simple, unrestricting and challenging.

"They called me in because I'm the best person for the job. They've been trying for months to get close to what has been going on, but every time they think that they have something, they come away empty handed."

She was staring at him. Her warm, trusting gaze never left his face. Her open observation made him squirm. He wasn't used to such open trust.

"I guess that I still don't understand why it was you."

He stuffed his hands in the pockets of his jeans and just stared at her for a moment. He was on an emotional roller coaster and so was she. But she was in this whole mess, too. She deserved to know what was going on and to make her own choices. The only question was . . . where did he start? He'd start at the beginning and David.

He gave up his pacing and sat down on the couch next to her, not touching her. He wasn't sure if he could get through it if he touched her.

"Three months ago, my best friend was

killed when his boat blew up." He fingered the scar on his face. "That's where I got this scar. I was watching from the dock as he pulled away and I was thrown to the planking from the explosion."

"Oh Jamie, I'm so sorry. That must have been horrible." She sat with her hands clasped in front of her. Her hair swung forward, shielding her eyes. Amber lights in her hair danced in the firelight. Even with her hair a mess, and in borrowed, bulky clothes, she was a beautiful woman. He couldn't remember the exact moment he had started caring about her. He couldn't remember realizing that she was beautiful. He remembered thinking she was understated and natural, but somewhere along the way she had become a woman whose beauty was incredible because of who she was, not what she looked like.

He gave a little self-conscious laugh. "I guess if anyone would know about loss it would be you." Even as he said the words, he wished that he could take them back. He had no intention of hurting Shelby by bringing up the past. They had enough to deal with right here in the present.

"I guess that I have become sort of a poster child for losing people. I can't say that it ever gets any easier."

He fought the urge to reach out to her. He wanted to hold her and take away some of the emotions running through him. But he couldn't. Not yet.

"Haven't you ever wanted another life? Why do you want to live with the danger?"

It was a question he'd asked himself a million times and had never found the answer. So much of his life had been trying to prove to everyone that he was good enough to handle anything. After a while, he had become the job, until it was hard to distinguish him from what he did.

He turned away, staring hard at the flames. There were other reasons he had joined, reasons that years of hiding inside had made him who he was. "It's quite an accomplishment, to do what I do. I'm the one that they send in when no one else can do the job. I wanted it to be that way. I was perfect for the job. I didn't have any real ties to keep me from doing what needed to be done and no one to distract me from getting the job done."

"But what about your family? They must be concerned for your safety."

He just shrugged. His family relationships were the hardest for him to explain. Even after all of these years he couldn't figure out for himself where he stood with his family.

"My father wanted me to practice law, just as he does. I was born to be the lawyer of the family. I was supposed to follow in his footsteps and be all that he wanted me to be."

"But you chose the ocean instead." Somehow, he knew that she of all people would understand his fascination with the ocean. He needed to be around it, or there was a part of him that felt like it was missing.

"My father was angry with me for a long time. I let him down in more ways than one and he and I have never quite been able to get beyond it." Once he started letting the words out, the panicky ache he'd been carrying around in his stomach subsided a little. He hadn't told anyone about his family for a very long time.

He got up, crossing over to the bookcase, and pulled a photo down from one of the higher shelves. He stared at it a moment, before moving to hand it over to her.

He hadn't looked at the photo for a long time. It had been painful, too painful to remember. Every time that he looked at it, the old feelings came back. And they were feelings that he had never been quite able to deal with.

"I said that I knew what you were talking about, when you spoke of loss. I do know what it's like. That boy in the picture is my brother, Sam. He drowned when he was sixteen."

"I'm so sorry. What happened?" He could hear the catch in her voice; the emotions just below the surface. He couldn't look at her, because he wasn't sure that he could tell the story if he did.

"We both loved to sail. We had been sailing since we were old enough to walk." He laughed a little as he remembered. There had been good times, but they had been very long ago.

"Sam and I couldn't wait until we were old enough to go out sailing by ourselves. My father had a little sailboat. It was nothing fancy, but we were convinced that we could sail it." He moved to the window. Telling the story was making him restless. Maybe he had just been restless all of his life. "Sam and I were only a year apart. We were as close as twins, but we were also as different as two people could be. He wanted to be the lawyer, not me. Sam wanted it so bad that sailing was the only thing that could take his mind off of it. But Dad wouldn't hear of it for some reason."

He moved away from the window and

chanced a glance at her. She sat stone still, staring up at him. Outside the wind was still howling and rattling the windows, but for some reason he felt safe here with her.

"We had come to Ledgeview for the summer and Sam had just turned sixteen. I was the big older brother at seventeen and I had just graduated high school. I'd been accepted into Boston University in the fall, but I didn't want to go there. I wanted to go to the Maritime Academy. As usual, Dad wasn't hearing of it." He picked up the picture again and looked at it. The image of Sam captured for all time, with a smile on his face that broke his heart. Why had it happened?

His words were pouring out unheeded now. He had spent a long time going over it in his head, but no one had ever let him say the words.

"Dad was still being a stickler about letting us go out alone in the boat, but we decided that we couldn't wait anymore. It was one of those summer nights that are so bright it looks like day. The moon was silver on the water and we couldn't sleep. We snuck out of the window and down to the shore. We pushed off the little sailboat and sailed out of the cove without anyone knowing that we had done it. We'd sailed all around the bay by the time morning had come. And we laughed and we talked and we just did nothing sometimes except stare at the stars."

He'd been so engrossed in his story that he hadn't realized she had moved closer, until he felt the soft touch of her hand on his arm. He turned, taking her into his arms. She turned into his embrace and wrapped her arms about his waist, resting her head upon his chest. He loved the scent of her hair and the feel of her against him. She made him feel all right, without saying a word.

"It was just about daybreak when the winds picked up. We were both happy floating there on our backs just looking at the sky. It came up quick and we shuffled around trying to get the sails set to head back in. But neither of us wanted to go back in. We knew what waited for us at home."

He moved over to the couch, never letting go of her and settled them both onto the cushions. The old soft fabric sagged around them, pulling them into a safe, soft cocoon. The top of her head was nestled under his chin; her cheek was warm against his chest. He closed his eyes and let his thoughts go back to what had happened. He had never fully played it out in his mind and gone back to the time and place. But he was going to go back now. Maybe telling Shelby could help exorcise some of the hurt that was still inside him.

"We were just turning to head in to the cove when the wind became fierce. We were off a small set of rocks out in the bay and the sky went from a heavy morning mist to darkened steel. Before we knew it the waves had white caps and we were being pushed around like a toy boat. The waves were getting higher and higher, and there was nothing we could do, but hold on. Before I knew it, the boat was tossed upside down and Sam had disappeared." His voice broke and she hugged him tighter, lending him some of her strength.

"He was gone just like that. I was frantic. I searched as best I could and still keep my hold on the boat, but I couldn't see him anywhere." He pulled her tighter, hoping to hold off the ache that filled him.

"I clung to the side of the boat, until my fingers were raw. I kept yelling and yelling for him and there was no answer." Her hand moved up to cradle his cheek. He could feel the hot wetness of her tears against his skin. But she still didn't say anything.

"I don't know how long I had been holding on, when the Coast Guard arrived. I couldn't talk from all the screaming and the salt water that kept splashing into my mouth. But I knew at that point that Sam was gone."

He was crying along with her now and he didn't care. He had finally told someone the whole awful story, something that he had never dared do before. Now, he would have to see if she judged him. He had put himself out to her and told her his worst secret and he needed to know if she would understand or pull away.

"I am so sorry, Jamie." Her voice was hoarse and her breath brushed across his chest. She didn't move. She just stayed there, against him, holding him.

"Oh, Shelby what am I going to do with you?" He ran a hand over her hair. He couldn't stand it any longer. He wanted to hold on to her, even if it was just for a little while.

The scent of earthy rain filled her hair and he ran a hand up to cradle her neck beneath the tangled tendrils. Just for a moment he allowed himself to close his eyes and store away the memory of holding her. He had a feeling he was going to need that memory sometime soon, after this was all done.

He pulled back, but only far enough so that he could look into her eyes. He kept her in the circle of his arms.

"I need to be able to look at this logically, Shelby. It's what I'm trained to do." He was going to be honest, lay his cards on the table. He could only hope that she didn't back away. "Right now, because of your uncle's past, he has raised some suspicion in me. He has a way of disappearing, just as he did today."

She pulled back, but stayed within the circle of his arms. "But my uncle couldn't be up to something illegal. I would know it if he were. Besides, he wouldn't do anything that would put us in danger."

"I wish that I had your kind of optimism about him, but the fact remains that he has more of a motive than anyone else that I have run across."

"What do you mean motive? What could my uncle want with smuggling?" She looked at him confused.

"Smuggling is a profitable business, provided that you don't get caught." It was a fact, one that he couldn't ignore. Many had fallen because of the lure of money.

She shook her head. "Maybe so, but that doesn't explain why you would think that he's behind the smuggling. Uncle John is such a good man. I've never seen him do anything that was out of the ordinary. It just doesn't make any sense that you would think that he was somehow involved in something illegal." Frustration reared through her slender body. Her nerve endings dancing beneath his touch. He didn't want to make her angry, but the fact still remained. Right now, John Case was as likely a suspect as any that he could think of.

The sky outside the windows was now pitch black. It must be close to midnight and the darkness felt like a shelter dome around them.

"How much do you know about what your uncle did before he came to Chandler, Shelby?"

"Nothing." She shook her head. "It never dawned on me to ask. He's a very private man. He showed up here one day out of the blue just after our father had passed away. I mean, we'd always heard about him from Dad, but up until the day of the funeral we had never even met him. And then, suddenly, he came to Chandler and said he was going to help us." She let out a heavy sigh as though reliving the past was weighing upon her.

He didn't want to put her through this. He didn't want to hurt her, but he had to find out what the connection was between

Case and the smuggling. "So up until two years ago, you had never set eyes on him before?"

She shook her head. "I guess it has been about two years ago, maybe a little less. After Dad died, Tommy didn't have time for the family business. He had his boat and traps and he was determined to make a go of it. Josh was fishing his own boat and he never showed much interest in the wharf. So, when Uncle John showed up, he just sort of jumped into the fray and helped out. We never asked him to help. He just did it." Her shoulders sagged against him.

Jamie wanted more than anything to tell her that she was through losing people that she cared about, but he couldn't make that kind of promise to her. Not when he knew that he couldn't keep it. They were at the beginning of something special, but it was still a very fragile thing. The right thing to do would be to walk away now, before she had feelings for him, before he could figure out what it was that he felt for her. But he couldn't walk away now, not when he was this close to figuring it all out.

"There are things about your uncle that you should know." She lifted her face from his chest to look at him. Her large brown eyes were confused and hesitant. He hated himself for the feelings that he saw there. Maybe telling her wasn't such a good thing after all.

"Such as?" She looked up at him. What could he do? He knew he couldn't tell her about Case's past. Not right now. He didn't have all of the answers himself and it wouldn't be fair to break her trust, when he couldn't give her the full truth.

He put a hand to her cheek and brushed away the remains of a tear. A tear he had caused. Her skin was soft at his touch as she leaned into the caress. She was a beautiful woman.

"I don't have answers that you need right now, Shelby. I wish to hell I did. I have questions about his past and what he did before he came to Chandler, but I don't know how it all fits into what is going on. I only hope that I'm wrong."

She closed her eyes for a moment. He could see and feel the hurt in her. She was trying to process it all, to take it all in and make it right. He just wished that he could do it for her.

"I know you will make it right, Jamie." Her words sent a small shot of electricity through him. She had chosen to trust him and that was worth everything right now.

"I'll make everything right. I promise."

He let his hand travel the length of her back to settle at the base of her back, pulling the full length of her against him. He felt her warmth through the soft fabric of her shirt as a shudder ran up her spine.

"We shouldn't do this, Shelby." But his words were just words. He want her, she could feel it in him as much as in herself.

Jamie trailed his free hand upward, his fingers touching at the strong cord of her spine, and pleasure rippled through her. He could enchant her with just a touch. It was an incredible power.

"If you don't want to touch me, I can walk away." Her words stopped as his lips came down upon hers. The kiss was urgent at first, demanding and needy, and she gave as much as she took. He pressed closer to her, pulling her tight against him with his hands. The kiss broke and she opened her eyes to see what had stopped him. Maybe she hadn't kissed him well enough. Maybe he didn't feel right about it all.

His eyes were like steel, radiating cold and hot at the same time. His eyelids were heavy as he peered at her beneath those incredible long lashes.

"I don't think that I will ever be able to walk away from you again," Jamie said, and, for the first time, she knew that what she was looking at was the real Jamie, the one who had told her about his brother, the one who promised to protect her.

"You asked me to tell you everything. You wanted to know all of me." She held her breath as he continued to look into her with his gaze.

"I've already told you more than I've told anyone in a lifetime. But right now, right this minute, I am going to love you. If you let me." His words were a pledge that she knew came from his heart. He was offering her much more than pleasures. He was giving her himself.

She raised up on her toes, trembling as she pressed her lips to his. She wanted him with an intensity she had never felt before. If she didn't have him now she was going to go up in flames and dissolve into ashes at his feet.

He let her take the initiative, watching her through those guarded eyes. She reached her hand up to touch the hollowing spot at his neck, her fingertips grazing the gentle skin at his chest. She had admired his chest before. He had strong, wide shoulders and a broad chest covered in sparse dark hair. His skin gleamed in the light from the fireplace as he leaned down to kiss her. She pulled back, stilling his movements as she shook her head. She needed to please him. She needed to see the effect she could have on him. Never had she felt the kind of intoxicating power that came with the ability to affect him with a touch.

Jamie let out a low growl that radiated from deep within his chest and she smiled. She was getting to him.

She reveled in her newfound power by exploring the plains of his chest. She ran her hands across the hardened strength of his waist where it narrowed to the band of his jeans, and she gloried in the sharp intake of breath and muttered curse as she explored.

"Woman, you are going to kill me. I can't stand it. I need to touch you." True to his words, his hands moved from the small of her back to nestle against the curve of her bottom, lifting her up against him, thigh to thigh, chest to chest, lips to lips. The storm outside had moved within her. She was hot and shivering and every part of her body was electrified.

His fingers moved to the buttons of her shirt, making quick work of the soft fabric, letting it slip from her bare shoulders as he bent his head, tracing the line of her collar with his lips. She slid her fingers into his hair, threading them through the dark heavy mass. He had wonderful hair.

He picked her up and moved to settle her in front of the fire. In her secret fantasies, she had dreamed of such a romantic scene, a beautiful fire on a stormy night with a man who could melt her with his touch.

Skin touched to heated skin as they lay in front of the flames. Each took turns exploring and enticing, touching and feeling and playfulness until they were burning.

"Tell me you want to make love with me." She needed to hear the words. She needed to know that he was feeling the same restlessness that was coursing through her.

He raised up on an elbow above her, running a hand down her cheek to nestle against her chin. There was no hesitation in his eyes, just wanting and needing.

"I've never felt like this. I know that it sounds like a line, but it's not. Somehow you have gotten beyond all the other places in me that I never let anyone else go."

He ran a hand down the length of her, following it with soft kisses. Her skin heated beneath the touch of his lips until she wanted to explode from wanting him. She ran her hands along his sides, feeling him shudder and reveling in the intimate power. He sighed, his fingers moving against her, touching, tasting and teasing until she thought her heart would stop, and time ebbed away around them.

Jamie raised up, nestling the hard planes of his body against her. The fire and the heat of their entwined bodies warmed them and lit their union in a soft glow. Her fingers gripped the corded muscles of his shoulders as he entered her and she watched the play of fire and emotion mark his face before closing her eyes and giving into the strength and beauty.

Never would she have imagined she would be in his arms, and loving the way he made her feel. And for the first time in forever, she felt beautiful and protected. And all because of Jamie.

Chapter Twelve

The rain began to lessen. It had gone from a furious drumming to a periodic wind-powered splatter that rattled the windows as the tail end of the storm brushed the coast-line. Dawn was streaking through the turbulent sky, but it was enough to tell her that they had made it through the night.

The fire was still going. The embers had died to a low orange burn and despite the lingering warmth she still had to fight a shiver from running through her.

She had been awake for over twenty hours now and the last few hours spent with Jamie were like a beautiful dream. The memory of his touch and her response had settled somewhere between the wake of exhaustion and the gentle glow of their being together. As strange as it was, being with Jamie had been perfect. She couldn't regret it. Not even with the threat that hung heavy around them. She was somehow fated to end up here, with him.

She turned as a cold draft swept the room. Jamie had returned with another stash of logs for the fire. She looked at the way his shirt hung open at his chest. His hair was rumpled and disorderly like a child and the dark line on his jaw showed just how long they had been here.

"I brought in more wood, but I don't think that we should put much more wood on the fire. We should be heading out of here soon. It's been safe here during the storm, but now that the hurricane seems to be heading out to sea I need to get you to a safe place and get back to Chandler to find out what is going on."

She felt guilty. She hadn't given Chandler much thought the last few hours. For a small moment in time she had allowed herself to forget about the outside world and her brother's disappearance. But now that the storm was abating, Jamie was right, they needed to get back to Chandler.

A loud banging sounded through the room. Jamie waved a hand at her, motioning for her to get down behind the safety of the couch. He made his way toward the door, careful to stay along the wall. He hesitated for a moment, looking back to see that she was out of sight and under cover.

Again, there was a loud banging, but this time it was followed by the familiar sound of her uncle's voice.

"Open up this blasted door. It's still raining out here ye' know." Shelby scrambled from her hiding place as Jamie let her uncle in. Case swept into the room with a gust of wind, the hood of his black raincoat pulled low over his head, his jeans and boots soaked from the rain. He shoved the hood back and unzipped the front of his coat.

"No one knew we were here. What the hell are you doing here?"

Case raised an eyebrow at him and then motioned toward Shelby. "I'm guessing that you've told her at least part of who you are. Otherwise, I doubt that she would have let you close enough for you to be so personal like."

Jamie stiffened as a slow blush crept across Shelby's cheeks. Case was right. The scene was very domestic. Shelby's hair was tousled; her lips still held the subtle traces of their kisses. His own shirt hung open and his feet were bare. Case was not a stupid man. He was bound to realize what had gone on between them.

He allowed himself a scowl. "Shelby knows who I am. The question is, how do you know?"

Case shrugged off his wet coat and swung it over the back of the couch before grabbing one of the candy bars Jamie had left on the side table. He unwrapped it and took a healthy bite.

"Rivard, you leave as big of a trail as those Miami idiots do. If I wasn't sure of who you were before, I am now." He went to stand in front of the fire, warming his hands, as he used a free hand to stuff the rest of the candy bar into his mouth.

"What is this all about? What are you talking about?" Shelby asked, sinking onto one of the couch cushions and clutching her hands in her lap.

"He's talking about my Coast Guard background." Jamie scowled some more. Case had somehow gotten the jump on him. Coming to Ledgeview should have kept them safe. No one knew him here. No one would have known of his connection to the house. Someone was all too aware of his past. If Case had found them then who else could do it?

He turned to Case, who had his own speculative look. "I am asking again. Just how did you find me?"

Case took a long second before answering. "Roe and John Henry told me that you had gone out to Marianne's place. They got worried when the storm came in and you hadn't gotten back." He spoke slowly, measuring his words before he spoke. "I went to Marianne's looking for you and that's when I found her." His words trailed off.

Jamie sat down on the couch next to Shelby and put an arm around her. She was shaking again and starting to shut down from overload. The stress of her brother's disappearance and the loss of her friend had taken their toll. He looked at Case and saw the recognition in his eyes.

"I'm sorry, Shelby. I know how much Marianne meant to you." A single tear rolled down her cheek and Jamie willed himself not to go to her, pull her into his arms and brush away the tear. But he couldn't. Too many things were up in the air. Too many things didn't make any sense and right now he needed answers . . . answers that only Case could give him.

"So you followed us here?"

Case gave a snort. "Nothing as simple as that, I can assure you. I have contacts, people who knew where to find you. Just like the people who gave you the information about me." He gave him a direct look, one that challenged him to deny it. He couldn't do it. He was going to have to take a chance and trust Case. He only hoped that his instincts didn't fail him this time.

"I couldn't get here until the storm let up some. The road is washed out about a mile from here and I just barely got the truck through as it was. But my guess is that if I made it through there, then the people who are after you can too and they can't be that far behind me."

"Damn." As much as he hated to admit it, Case was right. If those two goons that had come after him were the same two that had shot at them at Marianne's then they weren't about to give up. If he didn't know better he would have thought that he was the target, but that would be stupid. Why would anyone want to go after him? No one even knew he was in Chandler. But if Case had managed to find out who he was then maybe someone else had, too.

"Those men following you are two nasty fellows. I've been watching them for a couple of weeks and from what I have seen so far, what they lack in brains they make up for in brute strength and firepower. The question is . . . just what do they have against you?"

"I wish I knew," Jamie said.

Case kept his arm draped around Shelby's shoulder and gave Jamie a direct, pointed gaze. He took the look for what it was meant to be. Case was going to protect Shelby and Josh, no matter what.

And Shelby deserved to be protected. She looked so small and shadowed in the oversized clothes as she huddled next to Case. She was going to need Case there for her when this was through. Regardless of what they had shared last night he couldn't guarantee that he was going to be there to do the protecting himself.

"Shelby, dear, would you go into the kitchen and get me something to wash down the candy bar?" Case gave her hand a gentle squeeze before pushing her toward the kitchen door. When the door shut he turned back to Jamie. All the tenderness of his expression had disappeared and for the first time Jamie got a glimpse of the Case that he had heard about.

"Just whose side are you on Case?" Case gave a nod and then looked toward the doorway to the kitchen. It was still shut fast. Jamie knew Case was making the same decision that he had made last night. If he was to let it all out and trust Jamie then he took the risk of putting himself right out into the open range of fire. Just like Jamie, Case ran the risk of losing more than trust in this situation.

"I had just come to Chandler when things started happening about a year ago. It was just after my brother had died and Shelby was trying hard to hold onto the store and the wharf and make a go of it. I wanted to be there for Josh and Shelby. I needed to protect them. They didn't have anyone else and I had a promise to keep." He let out a heavy sigh.

"I bought a boat and started fishing part time and helping her out with the wharf where I could. But I started getting a bad feeling when I was out walking one night and I came up on two men pulling a trap line from a Bayliner at midnight off of the point. I managed to duck out of sight before they could see me. At first, I thought that they were just stealing lobsters, but when I saw what they pulled up I knew that whatever they were doing out there couldn't be good."

"Was it a small box tied to the end of the rope?"

Case just nodded. "It was too small to be a trap and nothing else could be explained for what they were doing."

"Are you still with the NIA?"

Case shook his head. "The National Intelligence Agency? No, but then you knew that already. I'm sure your information has already told you why I'm not with the agency anymore."

"Because of the bombing?" Jamie needed to press on. He had to get all of the cards on the table before he could decide on his next move. Even if it meant hurting Shelby. "And you were involved with the bombing that killed your brother?"

Both men looked up to find the stark white face of Shelby standing in the silhouette of the doorway, an empty glass in her hand "What? You couldn't have been with my father when he was killed. He died in an accident while he was in Belfast doing research. You told me that yourself."

Case looked down at the floor and held out his hands in frustration. Jamie hated himself for bringing it all up. He didn't want to hurt Shelby. It had never been his intention that she hear about Case's past from him.

When Case spoke, his words were heavy and laced with bitterness. "Your father was killed because of me. He died when a bomb blew out a pub. The terrorist group I was trying to break up had set the bomb for me and your father was killed because he was there with me. I was the target. I stepped out the back of the pub to meet an informant and the place went up."

"So you're saying that my father was a victim? That he was killed by accident because he was in the wrong place at the wrong time?" She was angry. He could see it in the straightening of her shoulders and the flash in her eyes. Maybe it was better that she got mad. She had lost and she had been lied to. Maybe getting angry was the way to get through the hurt that she was feeling.

Case got up and pulled Shelby into his arms, enveloping her in a crushing embrace. She fought his hold at first and then gave in, settling against him as the tears rolled down her cheeks.

"Shelby, you've got to understand. I never intended for you to find out like this." Case's voice was strained as he reached a hand up to stroke her hair. "You had just graduated from college and gotten married, and Josh was barely out of high school. It was best if you and your brother didn't know how your father had really died. He made me promise to look out for you."

"I don't understand — why were we told that he was killed in an accident? Was everything that I believed about my father's death a lie that I'm now supposed to just accept?" Shelby pulled away from him and ran for the stairs, taking them two at a time.

Jamie let her go.

God, it was killing him to watch her in pain, but he had to let her go all the same. Putting Shelby through this hadn't been his intention. But it was better that she know the truth. He knew better than anyone, that sometimes the truth was the hardest thing to accept. And that sometimes the lie or avoidance was better for everyone involved.

Case got up to follow her, but Jamie put out a hand to stop him. Case towered over him, his expression was a black, threatening mass that almost made him think about running. But he didn't.

"Shelby will be all right. She has a lot to absorb right now and accept. But she will be okay. Right now, you and I have to get things straight and I need some promises from you." He moved over to the coat that he had left discarded in the hall. It was the same coat he had used to drape over Shelby to keep her from going into shock after their wild ride through the storm. The earthy sweet smell of her filled his senses as he fumbled with the pocket and he fought to breathe. He fought to concentrate. He had to keep going with this for David's sake. He had promised and he couldn't go back on that promise now.

"I'm here investigating possible leaks in a

smuggling case that the Coast Guard is handling here in Chandler."

"Operation? There is no operation. Someone is telling you lies, Rivard. If Chandler is being watched I would know about it. I've been waiting to see what action they were going to take, but so far I have seen nothing. Not a single boarding, no observation, nothing."

"There has to be some activity. There is an ongoing investigation already in place. I was only brought in because of the leaks that were threatening the operation."

"Then you were brought in on a fool's errand. The only people aware of what is going on in Chandler are the locals and they aren't saying much." He was silent a moment before giving him a speculative gaze. "My guess is that someone wants you here in Chandler, for a reason. And I would like to know who and why."

Jamie shook his head. "My questions exactly." He pulled out the piece of folded paper that he'd found with the guns and handed it over to Case. "This was in a package of five handguns I found washed up on the rocks at the point. They were attached to the end of trap line that looks to have been cut."

Case unfold the paper, read it, then folded

it up again, handing it back to him. "It's an old Irish proverb, something about treachery and the betrayer."

"I know what it says. I had a friend translate it for me. But I was hoping that you would be able to shed some more light onto what an Irish proverb is doing wrapped up with five military-issue pistols and sunk in a water-tight container, weighted at the end of a lobster buoy."

"Military-issue?" Case was silent for a moment.

"I've seen this kind of thing before," Jamie said. "The guns are small, compact, powerful, and easy to smuggle. Those, along with the note, have me guessing that they are smuggling into Northern Ireland."

Case stood up straighter, towering over Jamie's six-foot frame. He didn't flinch. "Just an educated guess," Jamie said.

Case nodded again.

"Although, if I were you and I had the kind of background that you have on me, then I would be putting me at the top of the list of suspects." Case was anything if not direct. "Then again, I don't have any reasonable gain from this whole operation. Money isn't important to me and I've already lost everything else, except Shelby and Josh." He shrugged.

"How much do you know about what is going on in Chandler?"

Case settled himself back on the couch before answering. "I know enough to know that those two men sitting off of Hen Island are a lot more dangerous than most people are giving them credit for. The locals have discounted them. They think that they're just a bunch of rich people staying out in a summer home and maybe doing a little dealing. But they aren't the usual summer types. They're too shifty, too suspicious and too standoffish to be out there for a simple reason. They never leave the island for supplies and they never interact with the locals. In short, they are not what they appear to be."

"But if you came to this conclusion then how come everyone else hasn't?"

Case just shrugged. "I recognized them as the two men I saw hauling that trap line I told you about. As for everyone else in town, people in Chandler pretty much stick to themselves. If what they were doing was out in the open, then they would do something about it, but they don't go looking for trouble as a general rule. But regardless of what I am seeing, I don't think they're the brains behind this operation. They're too slow about their movements. It's as though they're waiting for someone to tell them what to do."

"And you think that there is someone else calling the shots and making the drops?"

"I do. They are particular about when they do their pick-ups. I managed to monitor a cell phone call made out there a few days ago. Whoever called wasn't too happy about what has been going on here in Chandler. He was upset about someone who had just come here and he was telling them to hurry up and pick up a drop that was made a few days ago."

"But if you knew that they were up to something, why didn't you report them? Why let it go this long without doing something about it?"

Case shook his head. "I can't afford to call attention to my being here. I put a bug in the right ear, but I kept a low profile for Shelby and Josh's sake. I couldn't risk someone finding out who I was and having the whole damn world coming after me. All it would take is one good investigative reporter to get a whiff of my presence and I could put Shelby and Josh's life in danger."

"You knew there was a risk with your being here. But you stayed anyway. Why?"

"Because I owed it to them and my brother. I owed them something that I will never be able to pay back, a family. And if that meant staying here and keeping low to help them, then I had to do it."

Case was telling the truth. Jamie could see the frustration in him and he knew how much Case had at stake.

"So if you aren't behind this, then the question would be, who is?"

"I don't know, but I think that this person is closer than we realize. From the beginning I've watched every move made. The worst part is that I think that Josh was somehow caught up in everything that is going on. I think he found out that they were more than a bunch of vacationers on that island and I think they realized he was watching them and went after him." Case shook his head.

"Do you think they have Josh?" Shelby stood in the doorway. Her arms were wrapped tight around her waist as though trying to ward off the entire world.

"I'm sorry, girl, but I think that they do. I got as close to the island as I could, but I wasn't able to find out for sure." Case got up and placed an arm around her shoulders, pulling her close. "Gut instinct tells me that they're coming to the end of this little operation that they have going. They aren't going to do anything to risk bringing attention to them, just yet. We just have to get there before they do decide that Josh is a liability."

"Josh couldn't have been involved in something illegal. He couldn't have. I would have known." She tilted her chin in defiance as she looked from one man to the other. Jamie only hoped that Shelby was right. It was going to be difficult enough getting themselves out of this without having to wonder what part brothers had played in it all.

"So, what do we do now?" Despite the strong gleam in her eyes, her voice held a note of pain.

"I'm guessing that they aren't too far behind your uncle. We can sit around here and wait for them to come to us. But I suggest we go to them."

It was almost dawn by the time Taimon and Caruso made their way to the address the old man had given them. Everything was quiet as they picked their way through the low scrub pines and oak trees that surrounded the summer cottage. Thanks to the storm knocking out the power, all was dark and quiet.

Taimon pulled his gun from his shoulder harness and pressed his back to the side of the cottage, the weathered shingles biting into his back as he motioned for Caruso to do the same at the other end of the house. Caruso edged as close as he could to the expanse of windows facing the water and peered around the corner looking for movement inside the house.

There was nothing. No lights and no activity, nothing that would suggest that anyone were there. Above the wind he heard the roar of a motorcycle engine in the distance. He scrambled backward, tripping over fallen branches, and as he rounded the corner of the house the sound of the bike's engine faded as they disappeared down the road.

Taimon came lumbering from the other side of the house, holding his side as he gasped for breath. "They got away?" he asked.

"This time," Caruso said, promising that this would be the last. Rivard and the woman had more lives than a cat. And the last thing that he wanted to do was to tell the old man that he had let them get away. Again.

Chapter Thirteen

They waited at the head of the cove for as long as they could. With any luck there would some anonymity in the few boats that were headed out to haul after the storm. There wouldn't be many boats out on the water, but they wanted the advantage of trying to blend in with the ones that were brave enough to ride out the lingering effects of the hurricane.

Shelby watched as her uncle loaded the last of the gear onto his boat. He hauled the air tanks aboard one after another and stored them in the blue and white, plastic bait barrels along the stern. The plan was to get her uncle's lobster boat as close to the island as possible without drawing any suspicion. If all went well, they would look just like any other boat out checking their traps after the storm and once they had the anchor set they could ditch the boat in favor of the diving gear.

"I figure that it's best if I don't ask why your uncle has this diving gear stashed here." Jamie let out a low chuckle.

Shelby turned from the dirty window of the fish house to look at Jamie. He was pulling on a wet suit that would protect him from the elements. The dark color would help to hide him in the early light. She watched as he pulled the tab on the zipper and shrugged his shoulders trying to adjust to the suit. He picked up his gun and placed it into a small, watertight pouch, attaching it to the straps and checking to make sure it was secure.

"You're pretty obvious in that outfit. If they're watching for you then they're bound to notice the suit, won't they?"

Jamie looked up and gave her one of his lopsided, slow grins that made her heart beat a little faster. "That's why I have these great yellow bib overalls to cover them up. Believe me, with these on no one is going to think that I'm anything more than another fisherman out there." But she would, she realized. She would have known him anywhere.

He grabbed a sweatshirt from the hook by the wall and pulled it on over his head. It was large enough to cover the wetsuit and the waterproof bag and still look natural.

Jamie hoisted the oversized overalls into place and pulled the wide, black straps up over his shoulders. He completed his outfit by pulling on his new rubber boots.

Shelby pulled a baseball cap off the wall and handed it to him. "Here, put this on. It'll help hide your hair and shield your face."

Jamie walked a little closer. The gray-blue of his eyes were intense as he stared into hers. He got as close as he could without touching, his breath was warm against her face and she felt slightly lightheaded at being near him. He had that effect on her, the ability to hold her without touching her, to arouse her with a look and make her feel safe.

"What am I going to do when you're gone?" she said with a laugh, but somehow it rang a little stale.

"We'll tackle that when this is done." He chucked his finger under her chin. For right now, she wouldn't allow herself to think about what would happen when this was over.

Jamie reached out, taking the hat. His fingers grazed her shaking hands, sending waves of prickling sensation through her fingertips. He leaned down, brushing his lips against her cheek and trailing downward to her lips, tasting and nipping in a seductive dance before he pulled back. She watched his eyes glimmer with a secret and his mouth curve into that languid smile she had come to cherish. He reached up and stuffed his hair under the old, worn hat. "Thank you."

Oh God, she wasn't going to be able to walk away when she lost him. Not this time. Not this man.

Outside, the low growl of the boat's engine hummed above the muffling of the walls. It was time. She watched as Jamie moved over to the bench and grabbed a pencil and paper. When he was done writing he came back and took her hand, slipping the piece of paper into her palm.

"After we leave I want you to wait for one hour. Unless you hear from me, I want you to call the number on the paper and ask for McAlvey. Tell him that I am heading out to the island and I'm requesting some backup. The coordinates are here to give him. If for any reason you are unable to contact McAlvey then get hold of Tom Kearsage at the second number. Tell him that I'm calling in that last favor he owes me. And tell him that I need his butt and plenty of backup as soon as he can high-tail it here."

He gathered her close against him. The

restrictions of the layers of his clothes did nothing to hide the heat between them.

This time there was no smile on his lips, only his penetrating gaze staring into her own, looking into her soul. He reached up and brushed a strand of hair behind her ear and she leaned against him. She couldn't help herself. As much as she wanted to tell herself to keep a distance, she knew that it was as simple as his smile to turn her heart.

Somewhere along the way her heart had jumped into the fray of it all and it terrified her. She wasn't sure that she was ready to risk her heart again — although, deep down, she wasn't quite sure that she hadn't already given it away.

"I don't know what is going to happen after all of this. If my instincts are right, then we may be walking into something pretty deep." She rested her head against his chest as his strong arms surrounded her. She could feel the rise and fall of his chest against the palm of her hand. A single tear fell from her cheek onto her hand and trailed down her wrist. She wiped it away. The last thing she needed right now was to let them see her worry. The door opened behind them and she pulled away as her uncle came into the small room. She turned away, wiping away the trail of wetness on her cheek.

"I'm ready when you are. The boat is loaded and we should be getting out there soon. I noticed Johnson is almost done getting his boat set. We'll want to get out there with the rest of them."

"Good," Jamie said.

Shelby could feel Jamie looking at her. He was trying to read her thoughts, trying to communicate without the words that neither of them could say.

Her uncle came to stand in front of her. He took her hands within his large grasp and pulled her to him, enveloping her in a hug that surrounded her and comforted her.

"I'll take care of him." His words were spoken low, just loud enough for her to hear. Unable to answer, she just nodded. He pulled back and used his finger to tip her gaze up into his. It hit her hard. She had been so worried about what was happening with Jamie and her that she hadn't thought about the possibility of losing her uncle, too. Except for her brother, he was the only family that she had left. All of a sudden, she was more alone than she ever had been in her life. In this one day, she could lose everyone left who mattered to her.

"Shelby, I know you're worried, but it'll

be fine." He tried hard to coax a smile from her and she struggled to give him the strength and reassurance. Her uncle frowned. "When this is over I am going to have to disappear for a while. I've risked your lives enough being here as long as I have. Once this all breaks loose and all of this comes down I can't be around for the end of it. Jamie understands this." He looked over at Jamie, who nodded his agreement.

"I'm not sure where I am going. But I think that it's time that I face my own problems and deal with them. When everything is settled I will let you know where I am."

Her uncle leaned down, kissing her cheek and she gave him a quick hug. "Thank you for everything. We couldn't have made it without you."

The fierce hulking form of John Case sagged a little for a moment as sadness crossed his face. "Gal, Josh and you are my family. I'll make sure that Josh gets back here no matter what. If you ever need me I'll come. I'm not sure how I'll know, but I will come."

"I love you." She couldn't help the tears that slid down her cheeks unchecked now.

"I love you too, gal. Don't forget it."

He turned and placed a hand upon Jamie's shoulder. The two men stood shoulder to shoulder and for the first time she was able to see that there were so many similarities between them that it was no wonder that she felt drawn to Jamie.

"It's time," Jamie said as he came and placed a hand on her cheek before turning and following her uncle out the door. The warmth of his hand lingered upon her cheek, as she tasted the salt of her tears upon her lips.

The sky was still a funky gray color with streaking clouds that showed above the heavy, wet horizon. He could see three other boats heading out of the harbor, checking lines as they went. The rough waters were making it difficult for them as the boats rolled and pitched with the rushing of the waves. Water sprayed up over the bow of the boat and Jamie's stomach lurched as adrenaline rushed through him. Case held the wheel tight in hand, fighting to keep the course as he headed out toward the island.

He wasn't sure what to expect. He never went in without a calculated plan, and a way to get out if it got tough. Most of the time he had a team of people to rely on, this time he was going to have to rely on

Case to cover his back. Instinct was telling him to trust the Irishman and that whatever it was in Case's past that had him on the run was something that he was going to have to deal with. It was his own destiny and right now, he wasn't quite sure.

He thought of Shelby, stuck behind and unsure of whether they were going to make it back.

The hardest thing he'd had to face in a long time was walking out that door and leaving her standing there. All of his attempts to keep his emotions removed from the case had shattered and this was new territory to him. For the last ten years he had been a self-confirmed loner who'd spent his life, so far, just trying to make sure that he didn't have to rely on someone else.

Recognizing that he wanted more with Shelby was way scarier than walking into a known dangerous situation. Right now, he only wanted to keep her safe. Even if it meant giving up the fight to find out what had happened to David.

David was gone. And if there was such a thing as an afterlife his friend was sitting on a beach somewhere with a margarita in hand, watching him and having a great laugh over the turmoil he had created in his life by falling in love with Shelby.

He loved her. It hit him like an explosion with enough force to suck the breath out of him. He couldn't pinpoint the exact moment. Maybe it had been when he had been fighting it the most. Whenever it was, the truth of loving her filled him with a calmness that he couldn't explain. He had always thought of love as all-consuming, blinding emotions. But what he felt now was an assuring calmness and bit of peace that he hadn't felt for a long, long time.

"We're almost out to the channel marker buoy off of Spruce Point. I think we ought to at least pull one set of traps so that we can look like we are really out here checking lines." Case motioned for Jamie to come up from the stern and reached over the side to hook the lobster buoy, running the line through the hauler, and setting the winch in motion to haul the line. As Case checked the traps, Jamie used the binoculars to discreetly survey the activity on the island.

All was quiet on the island, except for two men who were loading equipment into the Bayliner he'd seen earlier. It was the same one he'd seen near Marianne's the night she was killed, the one she had painted into her portrait. Marianne had pointed a finger to the men who killed her without realizing that she was doing it.

Jamie braced his feet as the boat rolled again with the waves and looked back at Case who was busy pretending to bait the last trap on the line. He had thrown the catch overboard so that they wouldn't be kept on the boat when they bailed. It could be a while before someone came back for the boat. Hopefully, their little act would look convincing to anyone watching from a distance.

"They're loading their boat. It looks like they're planning on leaving."

Case gave a look through the binoculars. "My guess is that they realize that they've compromised what they were doing and that we're onto them. If I were them, I'd be bailing out, too."

As they watched, one of the men started the Bayliner up and pulled away from the shore, heading across to the north side of the harbor and out toward the point.

"I'm betting that they'll use the point again to drop their stuff. With very few people out there at this time of year they should be able to get out without any much notice," Jamie said.

Case slapped him on the back. "It's show-time. Are you ready?"

Jamie had his doubts, but the instincts that he had always relied on were screaming at him now. All of the so-called coincidences that had brought him to Chandler were like neon signs in his mind and right now all of them had arrows pointing in the opposite direction of where they were headed. He thought of David and what a thrill he would have gotten out of this case. He knew that there was more than David's death hanging on him going in there. He had Shelby and Josh and Case relying on him to set things straight.

"I'm as ready as I'll ever be." He took a deep steadying breath. "Let's go for it."

Case put a hand to his shoulder. Jamie looked up to see the concern on his face. "I want you to promise me that when this is over, that you'll take care of her." When Jamie started to protest, Case held up a hand to stop him.

"Boy, if you don't know your own feelings by now, then it isn't my place to tell you. But what I am telling you is that you need to make sure that she is going to be okay for me. I can't be there to do it, so I'm relying on you to see this to an end."

"Don't worry about Shelby. I'll make sure that she's all right."

Case nodded. Then he turned and started turning the wheel to bring the boat around.

Jamie faced the boat so that the view of

the stern was shielded from the island. It was hard to hold the position with the force of the white caps that were pushing at the boat, but within seconds they had both stripped out of the extra clothing and pulled out the diving gear and tanks.

"We should be able to get ourselves over to that small cove off toward the back of the island, just below the house. If we get split up then we meet just beyond that group of rocks that heads up the trail." Jamie nodded in agreement.

Case checked his own gun and slid it into the small waterproof pouch he had fixed around his waist.

Jamie slid his feet into the flippers and put on the mask and breathing apparatus. He looked over at Case who had done the same and was giving him a ready signal.

It was now or never. He gave one last thought to Shelby before sliding off the edge of the boat and into the water.

Caruso watched as Taimon headed the boat out across the short distance to the point. The high waves pitched and rolled the small boat, tossing it around like a play toy. Better Taimon than him. He was green just watching him try to keep the boat on course.

They had seen a couple of lobster boats

out this morning so far, but nothing to alarm them. Anybody still out after last night's storm had to be an idiot.

Their truck was parked in the bushes on the point, ready to haul their gear out. Only one more load and they were done. Once they sunk the boat there would be nothing left to connect them to the guns, or to the smuggling. The only loose tie was Rivard and the last shipment that had disappeared. With any luck, that lost shipment was sunk so far below the water line that it wouldn't show up for years. Or at least until they were long gone.

Normally, these loose ends would have bothered Caruso. He was a man who prided himself on getting a job done without failure. But Rivard wasn't his problem anymore. In a couple of hours he would be on his way out of Maine and back to warmer weather. With the money that they had made he could sit back for a while, maybe take an extended vacation on a small tropical island with plenty of sun and beautiful women to keep him company. When it was safe he would resurface again with a new identity and move on to the next job. He'd done it before — he would do it again.

His only concern about Rivard was whether or not he was on to them, but he doubted it. Other than Taimon's screw up by shooting at them, there wasn't a damn thing that could connect him to what they were doing on the island.

And in a couple of hours they would be home free.

A boat was circling around a trap line several hundred feet off the east side of the island. He raised his binoculars and focused on the boat as it rocked with the tide. He could see the yellow of their rain gear as the men on the stern fought with the trap line to hoist it with the winch. The swells were making the fishermen's work almost an impossible task. Caruso shook his head. Better them than him. He'd had enough of the unpredictable Maine weather. He was no stranger to hurricanes, but he would much rather have ridden it out on his own home territory than up here in the Godforsaken, cold island.

He set the binoculars on one of the boxes and headed back toward the cottage, humming as he went. Yes, just a few more hours and they were home free.

Shelby looked at her watch for the hundredth time. The hands weren't moving. They couldn't be. It had been an hour and a half and still she hadn't heard anything.

She considered raising them on the radio, but she didn't want to risk endangering them just to calm her fears. Jamie had told her to wait an hour, but the minutes were passing along in chaotic torpidity.

She watched the fierce white caps push at the dock making it sway and creak, and a chill ran up her spine to settle at the base of her neck. She felt helpless and alone and she hated it. All of her life she had sat back and let things just happen to her. She had no control over losing her father or her husband. The ironic thing was that she didn't want to sit back and let life happen to her anymore.

If her limited time with Jamie had proven anything, it was that life was too short to take a passive position. The thought of losing him was terrifying, but the thought of having to live with herself if she did nothing about it was greater. She grabbed the phone off of the barrel next to her and punched in the number from the paper that Jamie had given her.

For one long minute the phone just rang and rang. She held her breath, saying a silent prayer that someone would be there to help. She was about to hang up when the line was picked up. The rough barking voice was a welcome sound.

"I need to speak with McAlvey." There was a long silence on the other end. For a dreaded moment, she was sure that she had been disconnected.

"And the nature of your business, ma'am?" The raw growling voice cut across the telephone line.

"I need to speak with him, now. It's a matter of life and death." She only hoped that she was exaggerating. "I was told that I was to contact McAlvey at this number. Is he there?" Again, the silence on the line was deafening.

"Ma'am, I'll need you to hold the line for a moment." She hung there on the other end of the line and glanced at her watch again. Now that she had decided to take action the minutes were beginning to fly by with an alarming speed. Something had to be wrong.

"Ma'am, I am the Officer in Charge. I must ask what your business is with McAlvey." Shelby hesitated. Jamie had trusted her to get to McAlvey himself. For whatever reason, it didn't look like they were going to let her speak to him. The question was now, who could be trusted? And who couldn't?

"Ma'am? Are you still there?" She could hear the tension crackling across the line.

"Yes, I'm here. Please, I must speak with him. I was told only to speak with him."

"I'm sorry, McAlvey is not here. But if you tell me the nature of the emergency, then I can help you."

This time the silence came from her end of the phone. She was going to have to make a choice and it had to be fast. Now that she had decided to take action, she couldn't turn back.

"I am calling on behalf of Jamie Rivard. He told me to speak with McAlvey. He said that McAlvey was the only one who would know exactly what was going on. I need you to find him. *Now!*" The seriousness in her tone was scaring her, but she knew of no other way to get the importance of the situation across to the man at the other end of the telephone line.

"Rivard? You know where Rivard is?" The officer's incredulous tone reverberated across the lines. "Ma'am, I need you to listen to me. If you know where he is then you need to let me know, now. He may be in danger."

"That's what I have been trying to tell you, but you aren't listening. Look, I'm stuck here in Chandler, Maine, trying to contact some man who is supposed to be in Florida. But you're saying that he isn't there. I have to get someone to help them out on that island." She had never been this exasperated or this impatient with anyone in her life. "He told me to call McAlvey to get help."

The voices on the other end of the line were muffled for a moment as if someone had their hand over the receiver, but she could still hear the urgency in their tone. God, even they were scared.

"Ma'am." The voice on the other end was hesitant. "I am taking a chance in talking with you about this, but I need your co-operation. McAlvey is no longer with us. He opted for an early retirement and has not been heard from since. If you are aware of the whereabouts of either McAlvey, or Rivard, then I need you to tell me where they are."

"McAlvey is gone?" Desperation rose within her. With McAlvey gone the question was who would help them now.

"That's it. I'll call Kearsage. He'll know what to do." She hit the button to end the call. Somewhere in Florida, there were some very confused men who were most likely swearing at her lack of cooperation.

She dialed the next number on the line and gave a silent sigh of relief when she heard the male voice answer. "I need to speak with Tom Kearsage. It's an urgent matter. I am calling for Jamie Rivard." By laying her cards on the table up front she hoped she could avoid most of the confusion the other call had generated.

"My God." The words were followed by a long string of expletives that were punctuated with the clunk as the phone was dropped. When the voice came back on the line the words were clipped. "Okay, where the hell is he? I've been trying to raise him for hours. Why the hell isn't he answering?"

"Are you Kearsage?" She wasn't about to take any chances. She had taken enough of them already.

"This is Kearsage. You say that Rivard told you to call me? He must have gotten himself into a whole barrel of trouble this time to have someone else calling for him. Has this got something to do with McAlvey?"

This time she almost dropped the phone herself. "I tried to reach McAlvey, but . . ." Her words were cut short by another string of expletives on the other end of the line.

"McAlvey has disappeared. He's got half the United States Coast Guard on his tail looking for him."

All she could manage was a soft "oh." She had no idea of where to turn now. From the sound of it, it didn't appear that Kearsage was going to be much help. "What do I do? I was told to call you. He said that you owed him a favor and would help if we needed it."

There was a rough gush of laughter on the other end of the line. "He said that, did he? Well, this must be pretty big if he is calling in the last of his favors." There was silence for a moment before he continued. "Whatever Jamie needs, let me know. I'll take care of it. I owe him that much."

The tone of his voice was enough to convince her that she was doing the right thing. Jamie had said that he could be trusted and she had to hope he was right. Time was running out. She glanced out over the water. There was still no sign of the boat, or Jamie. "He went out toward Hen Island to check out the cottage that the smugglers have been staying at out there. He's convinced that they have my brother on the island." There was a rustle of paper on the other end of the line.

"He went in without backup? The idiot is alone?" She thought about her uncle and the risk that he was taking by just helping Jamie and Josh and she knew that she couldn't bring him into it. She owed him so much that she couldn't bear to put him in any more danger than he already was in.

She chose to avoid the question and let Kearsage believe what he would. "He was planning on leaving the boat off of Hen Island and using diving gear to make it to the island without being detected. I was told to wait one hour and if I didn't hear anything, then I was to get a hold of McAlvey first and then you."

"And you couldn't get a hold of McAlvey," he said.

"No, they wouldn't tell me where he was. They just kept me running around in circles and demanding to know where Jamie was."

"I'm not surprised. By now, they're going out of their heads wondering where Rivard is and just how deep he is in all of this. From what I've heard things are getting pretty sticky down there right now."

"What do you mean?"

"I mean that McAlvey's hasty retirement brought up a whole lot of unanswered questions. And with Jamie's disappearance the rumor has been that they're wondering what he has to do with the missing evidence."

"They think that Jamie is involved with missing evidence? But McAlvey is the one who sent him here on a case. How can they think that he had anything to do with it?"

"Because as far as the U.S. Coast Guard is concerned, Riv-ard is missing, gone

AWOL, and McAlvey has disappeared along with some sensitive material and a sizable amount of confiscated firearms. Now, the question is, where is he and how does he fit into it all?" These were her questions, too. She trusted Jamie without a doubt. She trusted him enough to know that he wasn't involved with the smuggling. But she didn't know about this McAlvey guy.

She looked out at the harbor. There was still no sign of the boat anywhere to be seen. She'd hoped that somehow he would be here by now, joking with her and saying that it had all been too easy, but that wasn't the case.

"I'm sending out the backup that he wants. Help is on the way from Boothbay. He'll have to hold on until we get there. I don't want to miss any of this."

"But what can I do?" Helplessness settled in her. She had followed Jamie's instructions, she had done what he asked, and she still felt as though it weren't enough.

"I would suggest that you sit back and wait. You've done everything you can for him by getting a hold of me. Trust me to take care of the rest of it for him."

Shelby hung up the phone and stared out over the water. Now, there was nothing left to do but sit and wait. Just what she'd been doing all along. But now it wasn't enough.

Shelby got up and went to stand in the doorway, watching the rocking and rolling of the boats tied to their moorings. If only there was something else to do to help them.

She took a few tentative steps toward the gravel walkway leading to the wharf as the waves pushed and pulled at the heavy docking, buffeting it with small white caps. It must be horrible out there on the water with the remnants of the storm pushing them all over the place.

The water rocked a small wooden skiff that was tied to the dock.

She would have to be an idiot to think of doing it. And yet . . . For over a year she had lived with the feeling of and absolute uncontrollable fear of the ocean. Tommy's death had robbed her of the love for the water.

Adrenaline and fear surged through her and she took a hesitant step and then another out onto the rough wooden planking. Bile rose in her throat and she bit back the sour taste. She had to take control of herself and the fear now.

Every nerve ending stiffened and she closed her eyes and prayed, needing the strength to get beyond this.

A break in the wind stopped the constant

buffeting pushing at her and she opened her eyes. The metal-gray sky was outshone by the clear color of day breaking through the last vestiges of the storm. Whether it was intended as a sign or not, she would take it as one.

Pushing down at the queasiness filling her, she untied the skiff and moved to the back to prime the engine. It started with the first pull and she moved it away from the dock.

Sharp waves buffeted the small boat as she moved out, sticking close to the shoreline. The wind pushed against her and the cold seeped through the fleece of her jacket. She needed to stay focused and in control of the fear that was pushing at her.

She had no choice.

CHAPTER FOURTEEN

The cold and wind bruised his face, until Jamie was sure he'd never be warm again. They'd made the long swim together, coming up onto shore on the opposite side of the island, where the trees hung low over the water and there was a thick stand of pines covering their approach to the house.

It was impossible to hear anything over the howl of the wind and the rustling of the trees. The sky was a marbled gray and white as the last remnants of the storm bashed the waves against the shore.

Jamie motioned to Case, and watched him nod in response. Without a word, they moved into the stand of trees and removed their tanks and diving gear. Case pulled a tarp out of his dry sack and unfolded it. They stashed the gear under the tarp and a cover of dead brush and leaves, before moving together through the trees toward the house.

The short journey felt like hours, but it was only minutes before Jamie could see the large deck of the house.

He'd forgotten about the rush. He'd forgotten the flying feeling he got when he was walking into something dangerous. It used to be a heady feeling, flirting with the unknown, but right now he just wanted to get it over with.

For a moment, his last memory of David waving from his boat as he pulled away from the dock flashed through his mind. This was what he wanted. Wasn't it? He was doing this for David. It was what he had come to Maine for. But then, he hadn't counted on the case being quite so complicated. He looked over at Case who was hunched in the brush, not ten feet from him.

"Do you see anyone?" Case's voice was a soft hush that could have easily been mistaken for the sound of the wind.

Jamie peered through his cover, straining his eyes to see into the darkened interior beyond the bank of windows. But he could see nothing.

"You go left, and I'll go right. Meet me on the side opposite the landing."

Jamie nodded and then started picking his way through the cover toward the side of the house.

The house wasn't large, just a single-story cottage with two or three bedrooms. A piece of property this size on the island was worth at least a million. No small price for an ultimate playhouse.

Jamie came to the deck and pried back a piece of lattice sheathing around the deck. He eased himself under the wooden decking and quickly pulled the latticework back in place behind him. The smell of damp earth rose up to greet him. His fingers dug into the decomposed leaves that had been swept in by the wind as he crawled beneath the deck.

He was aiming for the space on the back of the deck where the lattice connected to the side of the house, when footsteps on the planking above his head made him stop. He crouched in the shadows and listened to the heavy footfalls above him. One person moving across the length of the deck — moving toward the stairs down to the ground level.

He edged closer to the side and peered through the breaks in the wood enclosure. He watched a man walk toward the landing, a couple of boxes in his arms. Jamie couldn't see the face, but he knew from the sheer size that it had to be one of the men who'd surprised him outside the bar. The question now was . . . where was the other guy?

With bulk number one on his way to the dock, Jamie began making his way back toward the other side. He let himself back through the lattice and edged along the side of the house into the bushes and out of sight. He caught a movement at the back corner of the house and stilled, until he realized that it was Case motioning to him.

The man did have a knack for disappearing into the woodwork. Someday he was going to have to get the whole story out of him. But right now they needed to get into that house and see if Josh was in there. He watched as Case slid his body down the length of the house until he could edge his way next to the window that faced out over their location.

Jamie crouched under the window for a moment, waiting for the best time when he could take a chance and look into the window without being seen.

Suddenly, a piercing noise sounded from the direction of the boat. Case froze then dropped to the ground and Jamie pulled back farther into the cover of the brush and waited for the signal to move forward. But Case stayed where he was. Something had spooked him.

He watched as Case motioned for him to follow his lead and they moved back along to the side of the house facing the dock where the boat was tied up. Two men came out of the cottage; their arms piled high with boxes. They bounded down off the deck and headed for the dock.

It was then that he heard it again. The ringing of a cell phone. And someone answering it. There was enough wind to carry the voice to where they were hidden. Jamie strained to listen, hoping to hear something in the conversation that would help them, but he couldn't make out a single definite word in the tone. All he could discern was that the voice was male, and direct.

From their vantagepoint, they could see the boat and the entry to the cottage. One of the men starting moving the boxes around to make room near the front and began checking the gauges on the control panel.

It looked like they were getting ready to pull out. That meant that they didn't have much time.

Shelby landed the skiff on the far side of the island. She had taken care to go way out around the island, hoping that it would look like she had no intention of getting close, then she cut the engine and drifted to shore. The last thing that she needed was the sound of the outboard motor alerting anyone. She pulled it up onto a small pebble beach that was shielded from the view from the house by a stand of pine trees and with shaking hands tied the boat off to a nearby tree, stopping short of kissing the ground for a safe arrival.

Her feet slipped on the wet rocks, as she made her way up the embankment towards the house. Under the cover of trees, the scent of decaying wood was overpowering and the soft bed of pine needles on the ground masked the sound of her steps.

She stayed off of the worn path, choosing instead to stick to the brush and trees that would hide her approach. She had just reached the line of trees surrounding the cottage when she heard voices coming from the shore. Picking her way through the trees, she looked out over a small beach. A red and white Bayliner was tied to the docks. And there were two men on board.

These had to be the two men her uncle and Jamie had talked about. She watched as they started moving boxes about the boat. If they were both in the boat, then that meant that her brother could still be inside alone.

Chapter Fifteen

Caruso was piling the last of the boxes onto the back of the boat when his phone rang. "Damn," he muttered, reaching into his pocket for his phone. He was hoping to avoid the inevitable.

"Yeah?" he said into the phone.

"I've been trying to get hold of you all day. What the hell is going on out there?"

Caruso ran a hand over his eyes. He was getting tired of having to explain himself. First, he'd had to deal with Taimon. The idiot was complaining about having to get rid of the boat. But, they couldn't leave anything behind to point a finger at them. The authorities would catch up with them fast enough as it was.

Now, he had to deal with the old man.

"We have everything under control," Caruso lied. He wasn't about to tell him that they hadn't managed to find the rest of the last shipment. As near as he could figure, the guns were at the bottom of the ocean. The trap line that the shipment had been connected to had been cut clean. The only thing that he could figure was that it had been cut with a boat motor.

"What does that mean?"

"That means that everything is under control. We've taken care of everything."

"Everything? I'm assuming that this also includes that little matter of Rivard that we discussed?"

Caruso was silent for a moment. He could tell him that they'd botched the job and Rivard was still on the loose, or he could lie and tell him it was taken care of, which it wasn't. He wasn't particularly worried about having botched the job. After today, his connection with his partner would be severed and Rivard would be the old man's problem. If things went the way they had planned then both Rivard and the old man would be left behind to deal with consequences.

He chose to take the vague route. "I told you that I always take care of things."

"Okay, whatever." There was an impatient edge to his voice. "I want an update on where we stand with the shipment dispatch. Is the courier ready?"

Caruso walked to the back of the boat,

away from where Taimon was busy straightening out the boxes. It was best for everyone concerned that he keep his change of plans to himself.

"I got the call a little while ago," Caruso said. "They're having a problem with their entry papers coming into Portland Harbor. Homeland security has things pretty tight so they're being held outside the harbor until their paperwork clears."

"Anything we should worry about?" The old man's voice was thick with concern.

"No, just a routine check from the looks of it. The *Céad Míle Fáilte* should clear customs soon and then we can transport the shipment to them." With a little luck, they would time it right, so that they were on their way out at the same time as the Irish freighter.

Caruso wasn't worried about the change of plans. It was a foolproof plan. Once the money exchanged hands and the guns were on their way to Northern Ireland, he and Taimon could also be on their way, leaving their so-called partner behind. They were heading for a decidedly warmer climate, somewhere south of the equator. Preferably, where there were people who didn't ask too many questions.

"Good. Good. Everything sounds as

though it is going as planned." The tone of the old man's voice leveled off, reassured by Caruso's report. "I expect to hear from you with a full report once the last transaction has been made."

"Will do." Not likely, he thought to himself. He planned on being long gone by the time the old man discovered that they had disappeared, along with the money.

"Fine. Once you deliver, I'll meet you on the island. We can decide the final cut and finish off any loose ends." The line went dead as the connection was cut.

Oh, he planned on tying up loose ends, all right. And one of them just happened to be his so-called silent partner. He reached into the compartment under the seat of the boat and grabbed a black box.

Taimon eyed it. "What's that?"

"Just a little insurance, that's all." Caruso patted the box, before taking it with him as he got off the boat and headed back to the cottage.

Case moved closer to him, keeping his back to the house. They were okay where they were, for the moment. With the first goon inside, and the second one on his way down the beach, they were just waiting for the right moment.

Case's voice was low next to him. "It's a might weird that he brought a box back in with him, don't you think?"

Jamie motioned in the direction of the house. "What do you think that they're up to?"

"Damned if I know. But from the looks of it, they are getting ready to clear out. If that's the case, then we haven't got much time until they pull out." Case reached into the waterproof bag he had attached to a harness and took out his gun. Jamie did the same.

"What do you think we should do? Should we wait around for them to pull out to investigate or take a risk and go on in?"

Case rested his head back against the shingled side of the house. "I think we should split up." He motioned with his head towards the dock. "Besides, I want to get a good look at just what it is that they are moving in all of those boxes out there." He patted the small, watertight pack that held his gun. "I'm going to take care of the boat. It'll be up to you to get in there and find Josh."

"Okay. Don't worry, I'll get him out." He reached for his own gun. "I'll go around to the far side where the brush is thicker around some of those windows. With a little luck, I can pry one of them open and boost myself inside."

"Yeah, well, make sure that you cover your butt before you head in there. These guys aren't here for fun. And if my suspicions are right about what is in those boxes, then they have more than enough firepower to blow us out of the water."

Despite the tenseness of the situation and the adrenaline rushing through him, Jamie couldn't resist a little chuckle. "When this is over with, you're going to tell me how you got into all of this."

It was Case's turn to laugh. "If we get out of this —" He pointed a finger in Jamie's direction. "And you live up to your promises, then you're going to have your hands full with my niece. You'd better take care of her, or I'll be back."

Jamie had every intention of making sure that Shelby was safe for the rest of her life. But first, he had to finish this thing. "It's a deal."

Both men sat in silence for a moment looking up at the activity going on around the cottage. The only thing that they could be sure about was that if Josh was in there they would have one chance to get him out.

As they watched, the men left the cottage again and headed for the boat. This time, the box wasn't with them.

"It looks like this is our chance." Jamie reached out to shake Case's hand. "It's been good working with you."

"Someday, we'll talk. I promise."

Caruso carefully tucked the contents back into the black box and slid the lid into place.

It was just a little present for his partner. Something to help him celebrate — with a bang. He chuckled to himself. It was a morbid sense of humor, but it was the only one that he had.

He set the box on the shelf in the pantry where the color of the box helped it blend in with the stock of supplies on the shelf.

He looked down at the kid who lay on the floor in the corner of the pantry. He was young, couldn't be more than twenty and he was scared to death.

"I guess you've figured out that it doesn't pay to be too nosy." He couldn't resist a little smile. This was perfect. Not only would his little surprise take care of his partner problem, but it would also solve the challenge of what to do with their intruder.

"I hate to do this to you, but I don't have any choice. Gotta cover myself all the way, you know."

The kid squirmed against the gag in his

mouth and the ropes that restrained him.

"I guess it didn't pay to keep an eye on us, did it? You should have minded your own business and you wouldn't be in this mess."

Again, the kid struggled against the restraints.

Caruso looked down at his watch. It was time to get everything together and head out. With a little luck, they would be right on time to meet the *Céad Míle Fáilte* and make the drop and pick up their money. Then, it'd be smooth sailing all the way.

He patted his hand over the little plastic controller in his pocket. There was just one more thing that he had to do.

Shelby watched as the two men talked for a moment, before going their own separate ways. The first one headed back toward the cottage while the second one jumped off the boat onto the dock and headed in the direction of the small beach.

Heading right toward her.

She crouched back further into the brush. She could try to back up now and maybe get some distance between her and the beach or she could just stay where she was and hope that she was hidden enough so that he wouldn't see her.

Somehow, the thought of going anywhere near the water felt like a cakewalk, compared to what she was doing now. What in the world had possessed her to think that she could just show up, unannounced and unprotected, and hope to help them? She was a fool. She should have taken Kearsage's advice and sat tight, waiting for them to help him. Now, she had put herself into the middle of it all.

But she couldn't sit back and do nothing. She'd done that once and she had no intention of doing it again. She'd already lost more than most people her age and she didn't intend to lose her brother, or Jamie.

Especially Jamie.

Loving him was so different than loving Tommy. She still loved Tommy, but he was a memory and she couldn't go on living with a memory. She needed more.

She needed someone to hold onto, someone who made her feel like it was worth it to get up in the morning. She had proven that she could make it on her own, but now she knew that she didn't have to. She just had to convince Jamie that holding onto what they had was worth it.

A twig snapped.

He was coming closer. She backed up, moving as quickly as she dared without making noise. She stumbled as her foot hit a root. Her leg brushed against the edge of something cold and hard. She pushed at the brush next to her and her hand rubbed against something underneath the brush. She pulled back a branch and found a hidden raft.

She looked again at the beach. The man was moving fast and he was headed right to where she was hiding.

It appeared that she was out of time.

Caruso was just making it up on deck, when he heard footsteps behind him. He turned, thinking it to be Taimon, only to find a tall man wearing a dark jacket, pants and a knit hat pulled down low over his eyes.

Damn. He stiffened as the older man walked toward him. He should have suspected that he would be here. It was too much to ask that the whole thing would go off without a hitch. "What are you doing here?"

"I take it I wasn't expected." The older man looked down at his watch. The sunlight glinted off of a pair of mirrored sunglasses. "For at least a couple more hours." He shook his head at Caruso. "You didn't honestly think that I was going to trust you alone with the payoff, did you?"

"What do you mean? I wouldn't cheat you," Caruso said, a bit offended, but knowing that the man was right. He had been trying to cheat him. He just didn't need to let him know that.

The other man just shook his head. He crossed his arms in front of him. "I would hope not. I took care of that little deal in Florida for you. After all, this is a partnership. I handled what you needed and you took care of what I needed." He let out a low laugh. "It's as simple as that."

"Right. Our deal." Caruso motioned in the direction of the boat. "We were just finishing up here. Trying to get everything in order." As brisk as it was outside, he could feel the sweat forming along his neck and running in rivulets down his back.

Change of plans.

"I wasn't expecting you until later." He watched as the older man turned toward the boat. It was loaded with boxes and Taimon was busy arranging them.

Taimon jumped out of the boat and onto the dock, before dropping to the sand and heading up the beach. The idiot didn't even have a clue that they were about to get busted. If he brought that spare boat out now, the old man was sure to suspect that they were scamming him.

"Where's he going?"

Caruso shook his head, "It's nothing. Just making sure that there's nothing left behind that can connect us."

"Good idea. I would hate to think that there could be anything to trip us up at this late hour," he said, and Caruso got the distinct impression that they were talking about more than leaving garbage behind.

Their no-longer-silent partner motioned in the direction that Taimon was taking down the beach. "What about him? Is he going to be a problem?"

Caruso shook his head. "No. Taimon is with me. If there is a problem, I'll take care of it." And he would. Trusting Taimon's loyalty was one thing, but the man's lack of brains had him worried. It would be easy to trip him up, if he was pushed. Too bad. He would probably end up having to do in his friend as well.

"Should we head inside? It's damn cold out here."

Caruso thought about the kid tied up in the pantry and the package he'd left sitting on the shelf. Maybe his little problem getting rid of their partner was going to be taken care of sooner than he thought.

But his gloating was cut short as Taimon

let out a yell that could be heard all the way across the beach. Both men turned as Taimon pulled something out of the brush.

Chapter Sixteen

Jamie looked through the window to see if anyone was around before using his knife to pry open the lock on the window. He slid the sill open as quietly as he could and levered himself up and through the window, taking care not to disturb anything.

He was lucky. No one was around.

He made his way through the house slowly, stopping to check out each room as he went. It was a nice house, simply furnished in a nautical style. It would be a great place to vacation if it weren't housing known criminals.

A prickling feeling crept up his spine. He put it off and continued on — he had no choice. He had to keep going.

He made his way back to the kitchen. Outside, he could hear voices in the distance and he knew that he had to move quickly. It would be hell to pay if he was caught now.

He opened up a door off the kitchen and

found a small storage room. The windowless walls were lined with shelves and stacked high with provisions. And, on the floor in the corner . . .

"Bingo."

Josh looked up at him startled, and he realized that to him, he looked like any other bad guy he'd seen lately. Even with all the time that he had spent in Chandler, he'd never met Josh face-to-face, only heard his voice.

He made the universal sign of a finger to his mouth for Josh to stay quiet, as he crept into the room, closing the door behind him.

"It's okay. Your sister and your uncle sent me."

Josh nodded in understanding.

"I'm going to get you out of here as soon as I can. You just have to hold on a little longer."

He watched as relief crossed Josh's features. Score one for Case. He'd been right about Josh being here.

The ropes were tied pretty tight and he began working at them, trying to loosen them.

From outside, he heard a shout and he knew he had to act quickly.

"Hello, Rivard." The chill that had been

creeping up his back shot toward his brain with alarming speed. He knew the voice even before he turned. He'd heard it too many times to discount it as a trick of the mind.

McAlvey.

Jamie jumped up, whirling towards the familiar voice, his gun pointed and ready.

McAlvey stood in the doorway. The regulation uniform was gone and even the relaxed Key West gear he had been sporting the last time he'd seen him had been replaced by a black windbreaker, dark jeans and boots. He'd put a black cap over his light hair and was sporting a pair of sunglasses.

And he was pointing a gun straight at him.

"Surprised to see me?" He took off the sunglasses and threw them onto the nearby table. "I have to say, I am surprised to see you alive." He gave a look of amused annoyance. "But then, you always did have more lives than a cat."

Jamie stayed silent. He had no idea just what McAlvey's plan was, but he wasn't about to give anything away. Thank God that Shelby was safe back on shore.

"I have a little surprise for you, Rivard." Jamie watched as McAlvey motioned at the doorway.

It took a moment for his mind to register that the large gorilla in the doorway was holding onto something. His heart dropped to his knees.

Shelby.

Terror filled her wide eyes as she struggled against the ropes holding her arms in place. A red handkerchief had been wrapped around her mouth to gag her. Her clothes were covered in dirt and twigs. It was his worst nightmare, come to life.

"McAlvey, what the hell are you doing here?" His words trailed off as he felt the barrel of a gun at his back. Jamie stiffened as it poked against his ribs and he glanced over his shoulder to see another man smiling back at him. Three to one. Not the kind of odds he wanted.

"I could say the same thing for you. I was told that you had been taken care of," McAlvey shot a look of annoyance at the other men. "You were supposed to be dead before I got here." He motioned toward the goon holding Shelby. "Put her next to her brother and tie them up. But make sure he's good and tight. He's not getting away this time."

"Let her go, McAlvey. Kill me if you have to, but let her go."

"I don't think so. My associates and I have

worked too hard to get rid of any witnesses. I'm not about to let you all go free now."

Jamie gauged the distance to the doorway and the chances of getting all of them out safely. It wasn't going to happen without a miracle.

"Toss down the gun, Rivard," McAlvey said.

Jamie threw the gun at McAlvey's feet. He should have learned to listen to that damned, premonitory feeling. It was coming up aces lately.

With Shelby set in the corner next to her brother, the larger of McAlvey accomplices went about binding his hands in front of him and shoved him down onto the floor next to Shelby and Josh. Right now, the only thing that they had going for them was that McAlvey and the others didn't seem to know about Case.

"I have to give you credit, Rivard." McAlvey still held the gun, but now that Jamie was tied he didn't bother to point it at him. "You've always been a good officer, one of the best under my command." He let out a deep sigh. "But you were just too good at coming to the right conclusions, and David had a problem with being discreet."

"Did you kill David?"

McAlvey let out a laugh. The sound rang hollow in the small pantry.

"Once David confronted me about the disappearing guns I knew that he had to be taken care of. But he surprised me. He wanted a cut of the action. At first, I thought maybe you and he were both trying to get in on the action. But he set me straight, said that you were too straight for this kind of thing."

"David became a liability because he was one more person who knew what your game was," Jamie said. It was all starting to make sense . . . David's boat. His cockiness the day he was killed.

"Exactly. So, I cut the fuel line on his boat and set a remote trigger device."

"You were waiting for us when we came in to shore that day?"

McAlvey nodded. "Once I had taken care of David, I started to worry about how much you knew. I never expected you to be so tenacious about investigating his death. I knew you were close, but you weren't the type for emotional ties. So, I figured that with his death you would just bury yourself deeper in your work and let it drop." He moved to sit down on a crate in the corner, as though it was a casual chat, and he had all the time in the world. "But you surprised me. You threatened to raise all kinds of hell if you didn't get answers. And I couldn't have that." He waved the gun around as though it were a pointer. "I had worked too long and too hard to have you foul up everything, Rivard. I wasn't going to sit back and let you blow everything."

A strange look crossed McAlvey's face, the look of a man who was struggling on the inside. Suddenly, Jamie knew that McAlvey was capable of anything to get what he wanted, including murder.

The only hope that they had was that Case would come through with his promise of a diversion. Three guns against one weren't great odds. He could only hope that Case was up to it. He just had to stall a little longer.

"So, your plan was to send me to Maine to get rid of me? But how did you plan on explaining my disappearance?"

McAlvey scowled as he looked over at his accomplices. "That was the plan, but these two couldn't manage to do what they were told."

Both men bristled at McAlvey's words.

"You were to come to Maine and mysteriously disappear, go AWOL. With a little help your body would never be found and you would never be heard from again." He shrugged. "It was perfect. Back on the base you would be listed as missing. Of course, I would let them think that the accident had screwed you up and that you had gone off the deep end. But then, you did your part by showing up on the base, drunk and belligerent. It was clear to everyone that you were out of control."

All of a sudden, everything made sense, the meeting off base, the promise to keep things discreet. "You wanted it to look like I was suicidal."

"Very smart, Rivard." McAlvey tapped his forehead. "You always were smart. I knew that if you turned up as a suicide in Maine, then they would figure that David's death, combined with your brother drowning, had sent you over the edge. And I would be right there to tell them how depressed you had been."

"But how do you know about my brother?"

Again, McAlvey let out a horrible laugh. "I made it my business to know everything about your past. Once I realized that you had a connection to Maine, you became the perfect scapegoat. All I had to do was do my research. Old newspaper clippings, it didn't take much work. I was leaving nothing to chance, especially where you were concerned." He motioned toward the other two standing behind him.

"I should have been more thorough with these two, though. I thought greed would be enough of an incentive to keep them on the up and up with me. Evidently, I was wrong."

"Hey, you can't say that about us. We've done everything that you asked. We picked up the drops and we made the transactions," Caruso said indignantly.

McAlvey turned to face the shorter man.

"I'm not as much of an idiot as you think, Caruso. I've been watching you move that shipment all morning. You, and that other idiot, were planning on running out on our deal and pocketing the money." They stood toe to toe, as McAlvey waved the gun around.

With his hands tied in front of him, the ropes fell over the pouch at Jamie's waist. He felt around with his fingers for the knife that he had stashed. It wasn't much, but it might be enough to stop someone.

Now, he just needed a distraction.

"If you are so smart, McAlvey, then you must know that backup is on the way. They should be here any minute."

Shelby raised her head to look at Jamie.

She'd forgotten all about her call to Kearsage. Jamie was brilliant; help really was on the way.

McAlvey's jaw twitched.

"I always said you were a smart one, Rivard. I should have known that you wouldn't come after me without some sort of backup."

She watched as Jamie shook his head at McAlvey. It was like watching a chess game, each opponent trying their damnedest to outwit the other.

"Taimon, go out and keep watch. I don't want anyone showing up unannounced, especially if he's telling the truth."

Jamie stiffened beside her. Out of the corner of her eye she caught the glint of something in his fingers.

"Let's just say that I knew something wasn't right. So I decided that a little insurance was in order." McAlvey's chest puffed out. He was feeling proud of himself and more than willing to share his success.

"Well, since that's the case, then I guess we had better get out of here. The last question is what to do about all of you?" He appeared to think for a moment.

Fear rose up in Shelby's throat. Maybe it hadn't been such a good idea for Jamie to push him. She could only hope that Kearsage got here with their backup, soon.

The short man turned, pulling a box off the wall above their heads. He opened the lid, showing the contents to McAlvey. McAlvey's eyes opened wide as he looked inside. "I'm going to assume that you had that for taking care of the first problem." He pointed to Josh. "But since you were so creative, I think that we'll just have to put your package to use for all of them."

Jamie interrupted. "So, you're just going to leave us here with that thing, McAlvey?"

McAlvey stopped what he was doing and looked at Jamie.

"I think that it would be best." He started to put the box on the floor again, when the sound of an explosion rocked the cottage.

Jamie's head snapped up — McAlvey stopped what he was doing and went to the door.

He yelled at Caruso. "What the hell happened?"

"I don't know." There was panic in Caruso's voice.

"Well, go find out, you idiot."

She could hear the heavy fall of Caruso's feet as he ran out of the house.

With McAlvey's attention diverted, Jamie lurched to his feet, the jackknife open in his still-bound hands. He lunged at McAlvey, using his weight to propel him backward. And then, a shot rang out. Shelby screamed as Jamie fell back against her, pinning her with the sheer weight of him.

"Damn it, Rivard," McAlvey growled. Gone was the polite manner she had seen before. "That was a stupid move. Did you actually think that you could take me out with a pen knife?" McAlvey voice resonated through the small room. "Too bad it was your last move. So long, Rivard."

Jamie's body slumped against her as he lost consciousness.

McAlvey was already running. The door slammed, shutting them in total darkness.

Outside, there was a rush of noise, followed by a deafening quake that shook the house.

Shelby scooted around, scrambling up on her hands and knees as she searched for the knife. Beside her, Jamie's breathing became more labored as she struggled to keep her balance. She had to find that knife. This was not how it was going to end. Not if she had any choice.

The sound of heavy footsteps outside the door sent her scrambling back toward the corner again. Light filled the room as the door opened and she squinted her eyes, trying to adjust to the brightness.

The first things that she noticed were their uniforms. Coast Guard uniforms. Help had arrived. One of the men reached down, cutting the ropes free from her hands as another pulled the gag free from her mouth.

Jamie lay motionless on the floor beside her. His eyes were closed, his face was a pale mask and his breathing was shallow.

"Damn you, Jamie. You aren't getting out of this relationship that easy. You can't leave me now that I love you." She leaned over him, touching his cheek as several men came in behind her with medical gear and a stretcher.

"Ma'am, we need you to step aside so that we can work on him." She stepped back, as they all filtered into the room and hovered over him, helping him.

Someone had freed her brother and he came to her, putting an arm across her shoulders as she held onto Jamie's hand.

"Are you okay, Sis?" She looked down at her own hands and for the first time saw the red staining them. Jamie had been shot.

"Please, don't let me lose him." Her words were as close to a prayer as she could manage at the moment. A chill ran up her as she watched the mass of apparatus that they were using to help Jamie.

She couldn't lose him, now. She loved

him. Things were supposed to be all right. They'd made it.

Firm hands pulled her back as the techs circled around and started working on Jamie. All of the voices in the room melded together, until the noise buzzed in her ears. She caught bits of words, but they made no sense. She heard the words: "boat" "explosion" and "guns," but the rest were a daze to her weary mind.

She closed her eyes, willing Jamie to be okay.

"Ma'am, I'm Kearsage. Are you the one who called me about Rivard?" Shelby looked up into the warm, brown eyes of the officer standing next to her. She couldn't speak, only nod. She followed his gaze down to where Jamie lay on the floor. Several people were working on him, trying to stabilize him.

He didn't look good.

"You've got to save him." Her voice was barely audible over the din of noise surrounding them.

Kearsage gave her a reassuring smile. "We'll do whatever we can, ma'am. I don't know exactly what happened here this afternoon, but it must have been one hell of a fight. They are still trying to put out the boat fire. I'm kind of mad that I was late for the party."

He reached into his pocket and pulled out a handkerchief, wiping at the tears on her cheeks, before handing it to her to finish the task.

He gave a little chuckle. "Don't worry about, Rivard. He's a tough one. He's been through worse." He leaned over Jamie and his words were loud enough for her to hear. "And besides, Rivard, you owe us too much to bail out on us now."

Chapter Seventeen

The sun was going down over the cove in a brilliant blaze of color. Jamie dug his boots into the sand and watched the show.

"Red sky at night, sailors' delight." He turned around at the soft words spoken over his shoulder as Shelby plopped down on the sand next to him, shoulder to shoulder. It was the end of the first warm day of spring and he couldn't resist the chance to be near the water.

"You've been awfully quiet today. Is your shoulder hurting?" She put a hand on his arm. The wound was healing nicely, but he still had some limitations to his use.

"It's okay, getting better every day." He flashed a smile and took her hand in his, squeezing her fingers as he held on tight.

He'd had a lot on his mind, lately. Not the least of which was how close he had come to losing her. "I was just thinking about how lucky I am to have you with me."

She reached up, placing a quick kiss on his cheek. He was getting used to the feeling of having someone around, someone who needed him. Six months ago, the thought would have scared him to death. But Shelby was changing his mind on that score, every day.

Now that McAlvey, Caruso and Taimon were behind bars and he had been cleared of any involvement, he had some choices to make.

Some were difficult, like what he was going to do with his career now. And some were easy decisions, like Shelby. He already knew that letting her go wasn't an option. He had married her to prove it. But it was his other personal relationships that he wasn't so sure about.

"What have you got there?" She pointed to the piece of folded paper he had set on the sand next to him.

"It's from my father." There was a moment of silence as he just listened to the waves and the wind. He was going to have to face this sometime. He'd already faced so much. "He wants us to come to New Orleans to see him. He says that if we don't come, my mother is threatening to come to us."

She sat up a little straighter next to him.

An impish grin crossed her face and lighted her eyes. He loved her smile.

"You're going to take me with you to see your parents? I feel privileged."

He reached over and kissed her, stringing his fingers through her hair. His lips touched against hers, moist and tender. The softness of her face and the scent of her filled him.

He pulled back, looking at her face. She loved him. He could see it. And it didn't scare him anymore.

"I wouldn't leave behind the woman I love, would I? Besides, I need your support to face my father again. He's going to be pretty upset when he finds out he wasn't invited to the wedding."

Her expression became serious, as she looked into his eyes. He tried to tell her every day that he loved her. It wasn't easy for him, and she knew it. But he knew he had to tell her.

He'd almost lost her.

"I love you, too," she snuggled closer to his side.

"Red sky at night, sailors' delight." He quoted again, as the last of the daylight faded in a gleaming haze. It reminded him very much of the sunset he had watched on the beach the night before he had come to Maine.

And it was a strange coincidence for a man who believed heavily in fate.

ABOUT THE AUTHOR

Having grown up on the Maine coast, **Teagan Oliver** knows all about life in a small fishing community and, with her semi-equal parts of Irish, Scottish and Welsh heritage, she never lacks for a vivid imagination and a strong family to support her. She now lives in the midcoast area with her husband, two kids, and an ancient cat. *Obsidian* is her first romantic suspense. For more information about Teagan and her books, visit www.teagan oliver.com.

The employees of Thorndike Press hope you have enjoyed this Large Print book. All our Thorndike and Wheeler Large Print titles are designed for easy reading, and all our books are made to last. Other Thorndike Press Large Print books are available at your library, through selected bookstores, or directly from us.

For information about titles, please call:

(800) 223-1244

or visit our Web site at:

http://gale.cengage.com/thorndike

To share your comments, please write:

Publisher
Thorndike Press
295 Kennedy Memorial Drive
Waterville, ME 04901